The Life of Polycrates
and
Other Stories for Antiquated Children

The Life of Polycrates
and
Other Stories for Antiquated Children

Brendan Connell

Chômu Press

The Life of Polycrates
and Other Stories for Antiquated Children

by Brendan Connell

Published by Chômu Press, MMXI

Published in March 2011 by Chômu Press.
by arrangement with the author.

ISBN: 978-1-907681-04-2

First Edition

Design and layout by: Bigeyebrow and Chômu Press
Cover artwork by John Connell
E-mail: info@chomupress.com
Internet: chomupress.com

for Sujata

Contents

The Life of Polycrates and Other Stories for Antiquated Children

Publishing History

The Life of Polycrates[1]

With them you too, Polycrates,
shall have immortal fame for beauty
as long as my song and fame shall last.

—Ibycus
—*The Oxyrhynchus Papyri*

Und wenns die Götter nicht gewähren,
So acht auf eines Freundes Lehren
Und rufe selbst das Unglück her;
Und was von allen deinen Schätzen
Dein Herz am höchsten mag ergötzen,
Das nimm und wirfs in dieses Meer!

—Friedrich Schiller
—*Der Ring des Polykrates*

---

1   DRAMATIS PERSONÆ:
POLYCRATES, *Tyrant of Samos*
PANTAGNOTUS, *his Brother*
SYLOSON, *his Brother, a Luxuriant*
ANACREON, *Poet*
ERIPHYLE, *Polycrates' Daughter*
THEODORUS, *Artist, Architect, Inventor*
TELECLES, *Sculptor, Brother of Theodorus*
ECHOIAX, *Cook*
PISON, *a Flatterer*
MAEANDRIUS, *Secretary*
IBYCUS, *Poet*
DEMOCEDES, *Physician*
HERACLES, *Buffoon*
BATHYLLUS, *a Youth*
POLYDOR, *Athlete, Marshal*
PERIPHORETUS ARTEMON, *Engineer*
EUPALINUS, *Hydraulic Engineer*
GENELEOS, *a Sculptor*
TELESARCHUS, *a Citizen*
ARISTON, *a Spartan King*
ANAXANDRIDAS, *a Spartan King*
OROETES, *Satrap of Sardis*
TELLIAS, *Soothsayer*

I.

Chronological Table

50th Olympiad . . . Birth of Pythagoras.

52nd Olympiad . . . Tisander wins at boxing. Amasis becomes Pharaoh of Egypt.

53rd Olympiad . . . Tisander wins at boxing.

54th Olympiad . . . Tisander wins at boxing.

55th Olympiad . . . Tisander wins at boxing. Croesus becomes King of Lydia. Death of Aesop.

56th Olympiad . . . Nabonidus becomes King of Babylon.

57th Olympiad . . . Ariston and Anaxandridas are kings of Sparta. Pythagoras invents the octave.

58th Olympiad . . . Polydor wins at the pankratium. Cyrus, founder of the Persian Empire, defeats King Croesus of Lydia.

59th Olympiad . . . Echoiax invents fish sauce.

62nd Olympiad . . . Cyrus dies, and is succeeded by his son Cambyses.

64th Olympiad . . . Death of Polycrates. Death of Cambyses. Darius becomes King of Persia.

II.

Sigla:

< > conjectural conceptions
[ ] uncertain reading
<< >> scriptural references
{ } offstage comments

III.

Aeaces ruled, together with its city of Samos, the island of Samos, that piece of land in the Icarian Sea, separated from the coast of Ionia by a strait, narrow, less than a mile wide. That tract of solid earth's surface, completely surrounded by water and washed by the sea, was for the most part level, but with its share of natural elevations, with Mt. Ampelus, and with fertile soil—figs, pears, grapes, apples and fragrant rose-apples, from that tree of greenish-albumen-tinted flowers, ripened there twice a year; its forests cried with peacocks, and low hills were spotted white with sheep, in places grey-green with olive groves; its circumference was about eighty miles and it had numerous pretty temples, to Zeus Ceravneos, to Apollo Nyphegetes, to Dionysus Dallius Anthestius and to many others, though most notable of all was the Heraion.

Aeaces had three sons, Polycrates, Pantagnotus and Syloson. Polycrates was the oldest, and the heir of Aeaces. He was handsome, had a strong, energetic body and though short of stature was among the best wrestlers on the island. He could swim well—to the Ionian coast and back,—run fast, throw the javelin a long distance, lift and hurl great stones—and he won many athletic competitions[1], was skilful at all sorts of martial feats, hunting, horsemanship and the employment of arms—and yet never bragged about his obvious ability.

Quick of comprehension, fully intelligential, from Pherecydes, the son of Babis and teacher of Pythagoras, he learned about the seven parts of the universe and the history of the world. From Phileus, the father of Roicos[2], he learned about the principles of the metal-

---

[1] He won the wreath of wild celery at the Nemean games.

[2] Rhoecus, son of Phileus, was a brilliant man, a great sculptor who worked in stone, clay, wood and bronze. In his youth he had dedicated a vase to Aphrodite at Naucratis and the goddess had since favoured him, letting him see with divine eyes the nature of both gods and men. He carved a figure of Night out of marble for the temple of Artemis at Ephesus, a figure of great power which, when seen, would make the viewer shiver and weep. . . . He had two sons, Theodorus and Telecles who, in their early manhood, he sent abroad to study art and architecture. Upon returning home Telecles immediately began accepting commissions for statuary, while Theodorus, still restless for knowledge, left the island once more. . . . Telecles carved a maiden out of marble for the temple of Aphrodite, a maiden more beautiful than any woman of flesh and blood. One young man, Xylocastro by name, fell in love with this piece of stone and on a certain night enclosed himself in the temple with her and fell to his passion as well as conditions would permit. Upon consummation, he left behind a Phocaean stater as the price of contact. The next day the act was detected and many in the community

lurgical sciences. His tutor in letters was the poet Anacreon, who worshipped with equal fervour Art, Wine and Love, and told his student about the affairs of Asia and his own rather ridiculous adventures [*as spear-for-hire, horseman, composer of ballads and epitaphs for sailors and the slayed flower of forces*]. He taught the youth how to play the magdis and sing, beautiful hymns to Artemis, Dionysus and Hera; and the subtleties of language, the various tricks involved in composition and declamation.

"Never invent new words," Anacreon said. "In public speaking never use strange phrases or antique words that have grown out of use, though both of these, in written works, are not only acceptable, but recommended and should be searched out with zeal; for the former shows you of original mind, the latter one acquainted with the classics and great authors, with Homer, with Pythermus. . . . Use noble words, an arsenal of words, exquisite words—treasure up old poems in your mind, for they will add to your compositions a patina of antiquity and to your speech force of expression . . . with which to forestall objections, ask questions, postpone opponents, marshal proofs and fill their gaps with padding . . ."

Later, upon entering his early manhood, Polycrates travelled. He went across the sea to Crete, the birthplace of Zeus . . . Cyprus . . . . . . visited Egypt, bearing a

---

called for charging the man with impiety, but the priestess of Aphrodite said that such a recourse was uncalled for, as Xylocastro had paid for his pleasure. . . . Theodorus visited Sparta, where he designed the Scias, the great music hall with its ingenious acoustical parasol-shaped roof.

letter of introduction to Khnem-ib-re, King Amasis, who served his guest wine of Thebes flavoured with petals of violets; feasted him on Nile fish resting beneath blankets of herbs, colocasium, and sesame cakes bathed in honey. Slim, smiling and silent young women fed him candied papyrus piths while groups of minstrels filled the air with exotic song, cymbals and the sound of the twenty-two stringed harp. The king took Polycrates on excursions to Crocodilopolis and Oxyrhinchus; showed off his building projects, his temples, of Isis, Philae, Edfu, Sohag, Koptos and Abydos; in Sais the magnificent gateway to the temple of Athena; and the numerous granite colossi, large man-headed sphinxes, criosphinxes and hierosphinxes, which great artists were carving at his commission. . . . Then Polycrates visited Babylon, where he was especially impressed with the sewage system and palace privies; the hanging gardens, the dazzling splendour of temple buildings, the shrine of Merodach . . . . . . fortification walls and paved processional ways.

IV.

When he returned home Polycrates found that his father had been assassinated and replaced by a hastily composed oligarchy, made up of the heads of the richest families of the island. The usurpers, in order to avert accusations of injustice from the populace, left the sons of Aeaces with lives unthreatened and a patrimony largely intact. Ambitious and desiring the power he considered rightfully his, Polycrates became a popular citizen by giving donations to the poor, who were naturally much more numerous than the rich. He gave fine clothing to the elderly, a meal every day to any Samian who wanted it, and, tearing down the fences that surrounded his orchards and vineyards, let the people pick fruit, figs, pears and grapes, as they wished. When he went out, he was accompanied by a servant carrying a bag of coins, and this man was instructed to distribute the money freely to all who asked for it. He also often contributed toward the expense of funerals, and lent his own couches and goblets, which were quite gorgeous and costly, to be used by anyone who was preparing a marriage-feast or extraordinary entertainment.

And, just as he had made himself popular, he determined to do the opposite to those who had diverted power from him, and stripped away the breath of life from his father.

His brother Syloson was in general a man of no great worth, effeminate in his manners and of lazy habits; but he had a certain skill in composing verses and silly epigrams; and over cups of wine the brothers would sit, Polycrates and Pantagnotus speaking harshly of those who had done them wrong, Syloson letting absurdities trickle from his tongue, bubble from his lips, which the other two would joyfully scribble down. . . . Then, in the middle of the night, the brothers would sneak through the town and paint these words on the walls of the most prominent buildings. Of Rea, the wife of Sarapammon, they wrote:

> Rea, see her jowls dripping with oil of land-snail,
> face plastered over with layers of white lead;
> fourteen sons have flown from her one womb;
> but none are squat, podgy like Sarapam-mon.

Of Hieronymus, who had prospered greatly by the destruction of Aeaces:

> Hieronymus wrestles with blind Aristippus
> in the humid shadows of the gymnasium;
> then shares his cloak with homeless Rha-damanthys,
> a stench worse than toad guts!

V.

The image of Hera, that primordial goddess, the genetrix of all things, was originally a plank of wood, a simple aniconic fetish, but later the artist Smilis, son of Eucleides and a contemporary of Daedalus, carved it into the figure of a woman of celestial beauty. . . . The maidens, with great care, bathed her in the water of the dark sea; then, on the pebbly beach, they dressed her in an apoptygma embroidered with flowers, tied a golden pendant around her neck and attached gold bracelets to her wrists. She was raised up, and under the orange-coloured sun carried to the Heraion. Nearly the entire citizenry of Samos, and many from Ephesus, Miletus, Icaros and Tragia followed behind, making their way in animated and serpentine procession along the twisted trail. Musicians clasped their lyres and pipes and walked with mincing steps; and choirs of bare-chested youths strode forward, songs going from lip to lip, describing in language rich with metaphor the glorious qualities of the bride of mighty Zeus, the great protecting queen of the isle;—all were prepared and ambitious for the musical and athletic competitions that were to be held later that day.

And then there were the mothers who, with garlands of lotus flowers entwined over respectably full breasts, led their children by the hand. And people of every age and station of life, laughing, murmuring, whispering: some faces grave with faith: old men leaned upon canes, tipsy from indulging in extra holiday cups: rich citizens took deliberate, pompous strides, their hair luxuriously braided and dripping with costly, sweet-smelling oils: militiamen, warriors of the city were there possessed of arms, to symbolically deposit at the feet of the goddess as offering: and Pantagnotus and Syloson bore spears.

"I never realised how heavy a spear was," said Syloson, shifting the weapon from one arm to the next.

Pantagnotus looked at his brother with disdain, and asked in an undertone, "Are you sure you are even able to use it?"

"Well, if I have to stick it in some poor brute's guts in order to get rid of it, I believe that I am quite able. It is such an uncomfortable piece of luggage . . ."

They walked with the people, followed the deity.

And she was carried along the reedy bank of the river Imbraxos, beneath the willows, and those tender and dripping branches tickled her face and figure; beneath the Lygos tree, under whose shade she herself had travailed; and to the temple, which was now surrounded by booths where small votive offerings and foodstuffs were sold, cakes of sesame and honey sitting in high stacks, pyramidical rolls of wheat, anchovies sizzling in hot pans and radiating a delicious odour, and small roasted birds full ready to fly down one's throat as if of their own accord. Fourteen oxen were corralled nearby, their thighs destined for the sacrifice; and the men let their tongues run over their naked lips or moustaches, for the remaining meat would be theirs, roasted to consume. Conspicuous was the great bronze cauldron of Colaeus, which was five feet high and endowed with marvellously worked griffin protomes, itself resting on three kneeling figures of carved marble, each ten feet high. The temple was filled with offerings; ivory carvings from Phoenicia; masterfully crafted small bronze votives from Egypt; cloths from Syria, Mesopotamia and Persia; Etruscan, Laconic and Corinthian ceramics; Attic black-figured vases; and thousands of terra cotta offerings from Cyprus. She, Hera, was set at the head of the high altar, besides which were heaped the ashes of countless former sacrifices. A vine tendril was placed on her head, by way of crown, and a lion skin laid at her feet.

Now women placed garlands of poppies and baskets of pomegranates, each rich in seed, before that goddess who was mistress of both vegetation and fertility, while the white-robed gold-decked neopoiai, the guardians of the temple, looked on and recited sacred hymns. Then the warriors approached, and each in turn lay their arms at the feet of Hera; but Pantagnotus, Syloson and fifteen of their followers hung back, so that when all other men were unarmed they brandished their weapons and in a body made a threatening cry.

Then Pantagnotus spoke, in a loud voice, his lips stretched back so all could see sharp white teeth set in blood-red gums. "People of Samos," he said, "for a long time now my family has been denied its rightful position, Polycrates, my elder brother denied his throne. From this day forward it will be otherwise, for Lord Polycrates, who the goddess Hera will always favour, has secured the city nearby, and we here who stand before you with sharp swords and spears quivering for seditious flesh, will take appropriate action against any who do not wish to live under his and our benevolent rule."

The people turned their eyes to the city, and saw distantly the minute appearance of men waving red flags at key points along the wall, and smoke rising up from certain locations, from those places where the mansions of the oligarchs sat. At this, several brave men of those noble families, Hieronymus amongst them, rushed upon the altar for their weapons, but they were instantly cut down, and their blood spilled over the white temple stones, Hieronymus pierced through the heart by the tip of Pantagnotus' spear. The majority however did not make any rebellious outcry, for they had been well treated by Polycrates, drunken the wine of his table, eaten the fruit of his orchard, their fathers and grandfathers clothed in garments delivered by his hand; so they voiced their support, chanted Polycrates' name, and those who were still opposed (such as Sarapammon) did not dare to openly show discontent, because it would be at the cost of their lives. So the sons of Aeaces came to rule Samos.

VI.

At the beginning Polycrates divided the state into three parts, Hesia, Aeschrionia and Astypalaia. He gave Hesia to Pantagnotus, Aeschrionia to Syloson, and kept Astypalaia for himself. But this arrangement turned out to be unsatisfactory. Pantagnotus and Syloson were both covetous of money, the latter because it could buy him luxury, the former, power.

Pantagnotus surrounded himself with a bodyguard of criminals, convicted murderers from Mysia and

Euboea, cut-throats who would hazard their lives for ignominy, profligate youth from home and abroad, young men who had squandered their patrimony on lewd female companions and fatty comestibles, who, through laziness, had barely kept from perishing from lack of food on their own estates and came to Hesia (which had become like a sewer) to make good pay by performing simple though vicious deeds. He stripped temples of their treasures, demanded gifts from all landowners, confiscated the property of widows, taxed and fined many citizens unjustly and had others put to death, simply to gain possession of their goods, and left their children to wander naked through the country-side, disenfranchised orphans; so Hesia, the territory that was his own, suffered as if it were under the rule not of a native, but rather some foreign oppressor eager to inflict retribution, to rob and humiliate the people. And his power grew. He gathered in stores of arms and armour and attracted more followers, paying for it all at the expense of the community.

. . . . . . he enjoyed watching flying insects kill themselves in a candle flame; he stabbed a man in Magnesia just to watch him die; throughout Hesia he placed spies and eavesdroppers; if a man spoke badly of him, Pantagnotus would have his nose slit or even cut off along with his ears.

In contradistinction was Syloson, who neglected his administrative duties and spent his time instead in the company of his various flatterers, catamites and eunuchs. Together they would drink wine from Scianthus and Rhodes, watch trained puppies from Malta jump through hoops, the gyrations of ithyphallic dancers, and nude acrobats balance in headstands on the points of swords. He shaved away his beard and had his face painted to look like the goddess Aphrodite; he began to use a depilatory ointment, made from four parts quicklime and one part orpiment, on his legs and chest; and, for hours daily, he soaked his body in a large gilded tub perfumed with essence of crocus. He would steep his feet and legs in Egyptian unguents, have his thighs rubbed down with thick palm oil, his arms with sweet mint, eyebrows and hair with marjoram, and neck with essence of thyme. Extensive sums of money were expended on dainties, imported ostriches from Africa, fat eels from Rhegium and almonds from Cyprus. And if all this was not enough, he violated the chastity of a virgin, a priestess of Athena Ergane, and subsequently had the audacity to have her buried alive for violating her oaths.

He spent his days in sleep and his nights in revelry, devoting himself wholly to his appetites. Sometimes he would stay indoors for a whole week, without once leaving his house, without once being touched by a ray of the sun. He did not bother with religion, philosophy, hunting or athletics but seemed instead to believe that manhood was made up of pleated cloaks of richly-dyed cotton and extravagant footwear.

He had a follower, Pison by name, an individual so small and thin that he looked as if a strong wind would blow him away; so diminutive indeed that Pythagoras, in a frivolous mood, had once remarked that, while all things in the universe are made up of atoms, atoms themselves are made up of Pisons;—and this Pison, this hypothetical particle of matter, who was in himself a catalogue of undesirable qualities, would, like some greedy shrew, eat daily twice his weight in food—comestibles smothered in rich sauces, sweet delicate things—whatever indeed could be found at his friend's lavishly furnished table.

The two sat together, in a luxuriously furnished room, on soft bags of cloth filled with feathers, wine-filled drinking cups and platters of delicacies placed between them.

"This afternoon," Pison said, "while going for a stroll, I saw a man digging his field, and the very sight made me feel as if all my bones were broken."

"Well," Syloson replied, languidly fingering a Phibalean fig, "just your telling me this story makes me feel as if an ox were standing on my shoulder."

"Which one?"

"Oh, I am uncertain. . . . Maybe the left."

"Are you sweating?"

Syloson bit into the fig, and chewing replied, "Possibly . . . if you see perspiration glistening my upper lip."

Pison's face assumed a look of great concern, almost panic and, without losing time, he cupped his hands around his mouth like a horn and shouted, "Iops, Zetes, come out you dirty slaves! Your master's lip is exhausted from labour, his person demands the breath of cooling fans of feathers!"

Immediately there was heard from without the hurried sound of sandals coursing over handsomely tiled halls, and a moment later two anxious slaves presented themselves, each carrying an enormous fan of oil-of-civet-scented ostrich feathers. Iops fanned Syloson while Zetes, a lad with dreamy eyes, fanned Pison.

"But tell me, will your chef be serving fried caviar today?"

"Pison, you are surely the slimmest of pigs."

VII.

Syloson was simply a fool; Pantagnotus was level-headed, cold, dangerous. For Polycrates, both were liabilities. In the middle of the night he had Pantagnotus abducted and taken to a country house where molten gold was poured down the man's throat; the next day he had Syloson arrested and brought before him in fetters of the same metal.

"Brother," he said, "when I see you here before me, bloated and drugged with cheese, I must confess that my disgust nearly outweighs my compassion. Look at you, with your face as hairless as that of a woman! This in itself is a gross and clear sign that you are on a campaign of vice and are involving yourself in activities inconsistent with a beard."

Syloson pouted. Polycrates continued:

"While pampering your vile body, living in a disgraceful manner, you have neglected all those duties which position and rank require of you. Your laziness has reached disgusting proportions. You have become frightened by the sun and live by night, like some lycanthrope, your blood inflamed by the moon. You live like a woman instead of a man, keep company strictly with men who are no men. I have even heard that you keep a fool named Pison around to help you chew your food."

"It is not true; I chew my food and he chews his."

"Syloson . . . you will chew your food still. . . . You will leave this island with your life, and gold; and yearly I will send you more gold, enough to pay off companions and stuff your paunch with sauced-up jays and foxes. But if you ever show yourself on this island again, your stipend will be terminated . . . and you will be put to death."

The next day Syloson was taken from the island in a small craft, frowning Pison[1] by his side, the gulls circling overhead, eyeing that latter, as if they might swoop down and carry him to their nests; and not long after, in Polycrates' stables, a mare was foaled with cloven hooves.

---

1   Pison followed Syloson to foreign parts, to live amongst the luxurious Sybarites, and then later they were welcomed at the Persian court.

VIII.

Polycrates married Xenocleia, the daughter[1] of Lygdamis, the tyrant of Naxos, from whom he obtained mercenaries; and he obtained mercenaries also from Bottiaea, Illyria, Crete and even as far away as Libya. He hired into his service hundreds of Sythic bowmen and Thracian peltasts, as well as many scribes, diviners, interpreters and skilled intelligence officers,—these latter endowed with full knowledge of hand signals, how to send messages by arrows, and able to disguise themselves as dogs, goats and sheep.

He levied troops from Myus, Ephesus, Priene and Icaros; and of course many from Samos, including one-thousand archers—always careful to have the number of his soldiers equally divided between natives and mercenaries, in order to keep the power of his armed forces evenly balanced and thus have a reasonable chance at suppressing rebellion from either group.

Around his own person he kept a picked corps of soldiers, those who were especially loyal to him and stood out for their skill in arms. These he equipped superbly with engraved bronze breastplates, and well-fitting Illyrian helmets decorated with crests of horse-hair, and trained and educated them for his purposes.

---

1 . . . who in turn gave Polycrates a daughter, Eriphyle. . . . Xenocleia, who on the same day in this world saw her daughter for the first and last time, then passed into Hades.

He made them learn the various principles and methods pertaining to the affairs of combat, and then study every noteworthy battle and coup that had taken place for the last five-hundred years. They chanted songs of war and blood, so their minds were filled with enthusiasm for battle. He gave them plots of land, presents of grain, silver drinking goblets and crowns of gold.

At meal time, before he touched a dish, he made sure that it was approved by his praegustator. His private secretary, Maeandrius, personally watched over the cooks and was under instruction to do all he could to make their lives happy so that they would have no cause for sedition. Polycrates had three properties where he would pass his time: his palace, a mansion in the heart of Samos, and an estate some short distance from the city. And in each of these, three times a day banquets were prepared, though the king himself would not let it be known, until the last moment, where he would dine. And yet sometimes he would dine at none of these, but simply appear at the house of a friend, or even some citizen with whom he was not acquainted, and demand a meal.

IX.

The island was covered with excellent timber, and with this he had a fleet of one-hundred ships built, obtuse-prowed biremes, each eighty feet long. They were constructed to act as both warship and trader, having every one a sail for speed—a single mast which could be taken down before battle and left on shore—and two banks of oars for docking and manoeuvring. Every ship was crewed by a captain, four officers, ten archers and a deck crew of sixteen men, which included sailors and carpenters, and then there were fifty oarsmen.

After drilling his soldiers vigorously in these boats, he plunged a chariot and six white horses into the sea, as a sacrifice to Poseidon, and commenced his naval campaigns. First he attacked the island of Rhenea, which, due to his numerical superiority, he easily overcame and forthwith dedicated to the Delian Apollo, binding it to Delos with a great chain. He then set out against Syros; the people resisted and, when he overcame them, he for the most part sold them into slavery or gave them, women and children, as gifts to his soldiers; then by assault he took several towns upon the mainland (Teos, Myndus, Pidyma); he attacked Miletus, an enemy for many years. The Lesbians (who had long boasted of the strongest fleet in the Aegean basin) came to their aid with forty-five vessels, light craft, with which they were able to thrust suddenly through the Samian line. Polycrates ordered his navy to surround that of the Lesbians, thus making their superior agility useless; and the Samian ships were higher, so their missiles fell more effectually; some Lesbian ships were rammed and sunk, some ripped open, some set on fire and burned, while others were boarded from all sides, the sea filled with broken oars, spars and carnage; and now no pris-

oners taken, them slain, perishing all, blossoms of manhood swallowed by the whirlpool of bright blue waves,
or some bodies washed up and dashed upon the rocks.
The Samians now turned toward Lesbos; attacked,
raided their harbour and sunk the rest of their fleet,
pillaging and setting fire to the cities, to Pyrrha, Eresus,
Antissa, Methymna and Mytilene (the reedy laughter of
children extinguished beneath the furious roar of war);
and they took away the strongest citizens bound, as
slaves, while demanding ransom for many others. . . . . . .
. After this Polycrates sacrificed an entire ship to Hera,
burning it to the ground in front of her temple.

He taxed all ships which passed through his now
greatly extended territorial waters, demanded yearly
tribute from those cities he had conquered and sold
protection to adjacent states. He committed acts of
piracy, by open force robbed valuables from all, made
no distinction between enemy and friend. "A friend,"
he said, "is more grateful if you return what you have
taken from him, than if you were lenient from the beginning." Under Polydor[1], a portion of his fleet attacked a
contingency of Spartan vessels and from them took a
huge bronze vase intended as a gift for King Croesus, a
vase of three-hundred amphorae, covered with figures

---

1   Polydor had the physique of a demi-god. In his boyhood he had trained
under Tisander, ate nothing but feta straight from the basket and cutlets
of raw veal, while never once venturing near woman or love-sick male. He
boxed with trees and wrestled with bulls. He took the wreath of wild olive
at the 63rd Olympics, won twice at the Pythian games and once at the Isth-
mus, where, to astound the people, he tied one end of a rope of white flax
around the prow of a ship, a fully manned pentecoster, and, with the other
end secured between his teeth, pulled the vessel along the entire length of
the harbour.

of bulls and lions all round the rim, and this was deposited as an offering at the Heraion.

. . . and the mothers of those Samians who had been slain in battle he allocated to the more wealthy citizens, directing them to take care of the women and look upon them as their own, while the sons he had buried at public expense, their names engraved on a pillar in front of the temple of Pallas Athena.

X.

With the newfound sources of revenue he brought enormous wealth to the island, and was quick to turn it to account, expending vast sums on creating prodigious and useful public works.

In Megara there lived a hydraulic engineer by the name of Eupalinus, who had gained great fame for building at that city an aqueduct and fountainhouse of wonderful beauty and usefulness, with thirty-five octagonal columns of poros stone and walls of limestone blocks in the isodomic system. Polycrates, with promises of high pay, invited him to Samos where, over the course of the next ten years, he constructed a tunnel to supply water to the capital city—a magnificent piece of engineering, a truly extraordinary feat—almost a mile long, carrying the main aqueduct, originating from a copious spring, through Mt. Ampelus. Eupalinus applied his geometric calculations and laid out his line (how difficult considering that from no place on the mountain could the two proposed endpoints of the project be at the same time seen). Two teams of labourers perforated the mountain, working simultaneously from either end. After advancing a designated distance, each team turned somewhat to the right. Then the northern digging team turned sharply to the left, in order to guarantee an intersection with the line of the southern digging team, which occurred after all those years, with cries of astonishment and delight. The actual channel for the water was then cut, with great accuracy, below the first tunnel and the internal surfaces were then covered with polygonic stone masonry and clay pipes were placed in a wide channel on the floor. The project was completed with over the earth works; water tanks, wells and channels.

XI.

On one side of the city was a bay, on the other a large hill; thus it was fortified by nature, and Polycrates did all he could to better these fortifications by art. Eupalinus constructed a mole in the sea, which went all the way round the harbour. It was nearly twenty fathoms deep, and over a quarter of a mile long. To design and oversee work on the city walls, Periphoretus Artemon[1], son of

---

1   Artemon was a short and podgy individual, who kept the black curls of his hair trimmed and well-oiled. He was very luxurious in his life, slept on cushions stuffed with rabbit fur and lunched every day on snails and deboned pigeons. When he was younger he had served as a mercenary under

Cyce, was called in.

Artemon invented machines that could hoist great weights; though once they were built he would only watch them work from a distance, for fear they would malfunction and their heavy loads fall and crush him.

the Persians and had witnessed first hand their tactics in siegefare, their battering rams, mantlets, mobile towers and great ladders on wheels. He had been caught stealing a piece of goose flesh from the general's tent and was punished, scourged and put to the rack until permanently lamed in one leg. Then, after having had every hair plucked from his head and chin, he was run out of camp, chased away with stones, abuses and cruel laughter. He lingered in Magnesia, lived off old vegetables and petty connivings in Sardis, and then, with great difficulty, made his way back to his native Ephesus wearing a hempen turban on his head, wooden dice for earrings, and a worn out old ox-hide wrapped around his ribs, looking strangely exotic, pathetically wretched. And he was in truth somewhat out of his mind, for he would cringe if anyone made a sudden gesture, when he drank anything it would always be in sips of seven and crossing over a threshold he made certain to put his right leg first. In Ephesus he kept company with bread women and common whores, beggars, false prophets and swindlers. Sometimes he acted as a procurer of custom for those women of relaxed virtue, at others the tout for moneylenders, or as a go between in the love affairs of married women. . . . Then one day the city, wanting to re-build its walls, held a contest for the best design, offering a prize of three talents of silver for the winner. Architects and city planners came from Halicarnassus, Rhodes, Attica and Thrace. Chersiphron, who had built the temple of Artemis, and his son Metagenes, who had joined with his father in authoring a famous treatise on architectural engineering, sealed themselves in their shop and laboured in secret. Calliphon, the Samian painter, who had recently moved to Ephesus to work on a piece for the aforementioned temple, was now said to be drawing up a magnificent plan of fortification on the wall of his own studio, while Zarex, a carpenter, built a great model in pine before the public's eye and let it be known that any man who stole his ideas he would personally sacrifice to Dionysus. But, in truth, every man in Ephesus, no matter how slow-witted, regarded himself as eligible for the prize. One could see fish mongers in the market drawing their designs on bits of slate and hear vendors of cheesecake discourse on ashlar masonry and axonometric projections as if they were accomplished draughtsmen. Artemon, in debt for a thousand small sums and as desperate as anyone, recalled his days under the Persians and all he had seen and heard regarding tactics. Having in fact an absurdly excellent memory he found his mind flooded with all sorts of details. He traded his turban and sandals for a scroll of cheap emporetic papyrus and set to work . . . . . . and when he was presented with the prize . . . . . . brilliant . . . . . . now wealthy, the fear of going hungry withdrawn. But this seemed to only augment his other fears, before which he was oftentimes almost panic-stricken . . . afraid of wasps, and the colour red . . . . . .

He had himself brought forward on a stretcher and in a reclining position he would examine the various works and engines that demanded his attention, lazily directing or upbraiding the foremen as occasion required. They would listen to his lisping voice with mingled disgust and awe and then carry out his instructions to the letter, for no man doubted that Periphoretus Artemon was a genius in the art of self-preservation. He fortified the city with over seven miles of wall, using a minimum number of angles, because angles, when all is said and done, offer a certain degree of cover to the attacking enemy, as upon their approach they cannot be seen by everyone upon the walls—and also battering rams can break angles with infinitely greater ease than rounded surfaces. The walls he built broad enough so that two armed men could pass each other with ease, and every one-hundred metres he put a gap in the wall of ten metres, which he had bridged with unsecured planks, so that, if an attacking enemy took one section of the fortifications, the planks need merely be pulled away and they could not advance to the next. The walls had thirty-five towers and twelve gates and loopholes were also built into them by which arrows could be dispelled. Around them slaves, mainly those garnered from Lesbos, were made to dig a moat in front of which palisades were built . . . . . . He fortified the acropolis . . .
. . . . . . Inside of the walls themselves a park was built. The walkways were first dug out and fitted with drains; then they were filled with charcoal and over this sand was layered, so that these paths were always

without puddles and could be walked on comfortably throughout the year. An artificial hill was made, with a corkscrew path to go up by. A great number of trees, pines and firs, were also planted in the park, not only for their shade and beauty, but also because, in times of siege they would provide a great source of firewood, a thing very hard to come by when the people's ability to forage is hampered.

XII.

Epistle:

Anacreon to Polycrates

To my Lord,

It is noontime now, and I have been up since dawn, writing rainbow-hued verses, verses dyed not only with the dark-blue juice of the vine, but stained with orange sunrise, green sap of emeralds and tainted yellow with the shells of frozen flames; and now with the same quivering pen I am writing to you, just to greet and ask after you. I long to see your face so very much! When able, I will have the verses copied out and send them on, and hopefully see you in person not much after that, for I am growing weary of Smyrna. Greet my Lady your wife.

Epistle:

Polycrates to Amasis,

My very dear friend Amasis, I am sending this packet of hymns by a most special messenger. His name is Pythagoras and he is one of the smartest fellows here in Samos, though somewhat odd, as he drinks no wine and eats no living thing, but subsists on barley paste, grapes, figs and cheese. For breakfast he will take nothing more than cucumbers and wild honey, while for dinner he considers sea-onions to be the greatest delicacy. But though rather mad in matters of diet, he still suffers significantly from the heat of brilliance, having made great progress in advancing the science of music and constructing marvellous theories regarding the fate of the soul. In any case, he is very eager to learn a thing or two from you Egyptians, so if you could have one of your scribes show him around, it would be most appreciated. I commend him to you my much-missed friend. By the bye: do you have a copy of Athothes' *Workings of the Eye*? I am most eager to get my hands on it.

Epistle:

Democedes[1] to Polycrates, greetings

I have just received your letter and,
though I have many pressing duties, am
now taking a moment to reply to one so
prestigious as yourself. That you are prone
to take chills I am sorry to hear. My best
professional advice is to avoid wandering
about your apartments with bare feet.

So, you want me for your personal
physician? Well, there is nothing I would
like better, provided that we can arrive at
a financial arrangement that seems suitable to my position in life. Before arriving
at Athens the Aeginetians paid me, at the
public's expense, one talent per annum.
Now that I am here, the Athenians pay me

---

1   Democedes was born in Croton. His father was a physician, a despotic
man who daily treated his son to both verbal and physical abuse. Democedes at last found himself unable to tolerate the quotidian curses and heavy
slaps that fell to him and so, in the dead of night, left the house and walked
to the city of Aegina. Even though he was without implements or any stock
of medicine, he was determined to make a living. He therefore stood in the
market and offered cures, telling the people that they need not pay him
before, but only after his advice had been given and only if they found it
effective. By simply applying pressure with his hands he was often able to
remove people's pains and his counsel always produced positive results. He
cured a man of the colic by telling him to let a live duck dance on his belly,
and cured a woman of inflammation of the eyes by having her tie the eye of
a myrus-fish to her forehead. . . . So he made a reputation for himself.

a hundred minae. So you might ponder what sort of offer you are willing to make to seduce me from this beautiful and noble city, where I am by no means discontent.

Epistle:

Polycrates to Democedes, greetings

I will not make you yawn with a long prologue. Come at once, I have aching toes on my left foot. Two talents await you, best of Crotonian physicians.

Epistle:

Polycrates to Anacreon,

Hail, my master

Are you yet familiar with the works of Hipponax? He, with his limping iambics, is all the rage in Ephesus right now: I have heard that he is quite deformed and his verses speak much about his obviously malicious disposition. Do you know of the Chian sculptors, those sons of Archermus[2], Athenis and Bupalos? The latter did some wonderful Graces for the sanctu-

---

2   Archermus and his own father Michiades carved a Nike for Delos, and in so doing were the first artists to give wings to that goddess.

ary of the vengeance at Smyrna and some others which are at Pergamon in the bridal chamber of Adonis. He is also known for a few temples he has built, many wonderful sculptures of animals and a heavily-draped statue of Fortune with a sphere on her head and one hand holding Amaltheia's horn. Well, in any case, these two seem to have taken it into their heads to caricature Hipponax, who promptly revenged himself by issuing a series of satires so acrasscent that the brothers have reportedly hung themselves, as Lycambes and his daughters did when assailed by the sharp pen of Archilocus. I have sent Maeandrius out to try and procure me a copy of these verses against Bupalos and Athenis, as I am eager to read them. I cannot deny that his poems have a certain coarseness of thought and feeling, and that his vocabulary is somewhat rude, but I do believe that his originality of expression and metre, his sheer genius, override these faults and that he is not a poet who one needs to make excuses for.

Epistle:

Heracles, buffoon, to Maeandrius, secretary

Health to you, honoured one, and twice that much health to your master!

While at the agora at Colophon, and while eating figs, I read your tablet, your advertisement in search of a comedian, and so emboldened, it is to you now I do apply regarding employment under Polycrates, full ready to offer all the secrets of my person for his personal pleasure and ready to demonstrate, both bodily and verbally, my ability at any time convenient for yourself those skills which are in a small part listed below:

a) Of humour I have countless succinct and jolly witticisms, most precious, and am often able to live for months on the power of a single joke. I am in possession of twenty more than twelve-hundred Attic jokes and never need have recourse to those from Rhodes. Impromptu, I can make jokes about bald men and then men of Cyme. In my possession are sundry amusing, very original doctor jokes.

b) I speak and behave playfully and in a merry way.

c) I can compare any man's face to that of the particular animal that suits him, and thereby cause amusement.

d) When it comes to telling riddles, I do not exaggerate when I say that there

is none better than myself, and never has
been since the time of Necho, that pygmy
clown of the Pharaoh Dadkeri-Assi.

e) I give an imitation of a cyclops trying
to sing.

f) I can ingurgitate a pigeon at a mouth-
ful and forty duck eggs in rapid succession.

g) I am a dwarf of ridiculous appearance
and am skilled at humorous body language
to match all occasions.

h) I am a eunuch and therefore can be
trusted around both wives and daughters;
though, like a gelded charger I am far from
lacking spirit.

i) I know many tricks, such as how
to make a man's face turn green, how to
make your guests' urine phosphorescent,
and how, with a tincture of coloquintida,
to make it so everything they put in their
mouths tastes harsh and disagreeably acrid
like wormwood.

In sum: whether it be engaging in japes,
down-to-earth leg-pullings or quips, deal-
ing out pranks or weighty hilarity, you will
not find one more skilled, search you from
Caria to Euboea, scrounge through distant
Thrace or far away Carmania.

I eagerly await your response.

Epistle:

Anacreon to Polycrates {in the handwriting of the former's anagnostes}

To my Lord,

You have given me an exposition on Hipponax and asked if I have heard of him.
The answer is in the affirmative, for he is
the author of that piece which begins with
the line 'Very little wit have men who dine
on drink'. But he himself does not possess
keen perception and cleverly apt expression of those connections between ideas
which awaken amusement and pleasure in
the least and, to tell the truth, I am rather
shocked that you should have become such
a fan of his. Simply because he substitutes
a spondee for the final iambus of an iambic
senarius does not make him a genius. He
uses vulgar language. Will you, whose sen-
sibilities I have always considered to be
more delicate than the rose, be angry if
I say that he is just a fad? And then, my
Lord, I understand the interest you might
feel in these brothers, Athenis and Bupalos,
hanging themselves, but of what use is it to
then catalogue the various works of art of
the latter? Do you not know that the surest
way to bore your reader is to tell him everything? Have I not often told you that less

is more? And the word acrasscent, which you use with such authority. Where did you find it, as I have never known any of the old authors to use it, or for that matter any modern? Or yet is it merely a quaint spelling of some common word, as when Sappho uses 'zapaton' for 'diabaton'? In either case, better if you stick to the old vintage. Furthermore, you should not say 'make excuses' but rather 'apologetic' just as one should not say 'make speech' but rather 'perorate' and instead of using 'make parallels' use 'collimate'. But to conclude, talking about the niceties of language when the subject is Hipponax is in itself absurd, and not unlike serving lentils seasoned with myrrh oil.

XIII.

The palace of Polycrates, the roof covered with quasi-translucent Pentalic stone tiles from Naxos, was splendidly decorated, the floors of certain chambers interlaid with precious stones and agate, others with extravagant mosaics, the walls of all painted with a hundred interesting scenes. One room was frescoed like an ocean deep, with octopuses, urchins, lantern-fish and dolphins, tritons, nereides and sea-dragons. Another had diverse birds of the air admirably depicted flying across wall and ceiling, perched on branches and pecking or scratching at the earth. There was a chamber which displayed scenes from the *Cypria* of Stasinus, another with scenes from Aesop's fables. In his room of oddities he had a stuffed hippopotamus, the skeleton of a winged snake, and jars, one containing an enormous and misshapen foetus, another the embalmed body of Hieronymus, a kind of memorabilia of Polycrates' rise to power. In his courtyards he had statues of athletes, satyrs, a naked woman playing a flute, an acrobat, a bull, a drunken old woman stumbling, a portrait of Anacreon.

On leisure days he would sit in his garden, under the shade of the amamaxudes, or else wander along the paths, sniff at the flowers and sample prime pieces of fruit from his orchard. There were roses that were half white and half red and vines which carried both white and black grapes together, grapes that were not fit for wine, but for eating were deliciously sweet. He had a mulberry tree which was grafted to a chestnut tree, a chestnut tree grafted to a hazelnut tree and a pomegranate grafted to an oak. He grew cadmium-yellow lemons which smelled of cinnamon, melons odiferous as peach blossoms, and artichokes which breathed the aroma of hyacinth, were without sharp prickles and tasted not unlike sweet plums. There were peach and cherry trees that produced fruit without pit and almond trees whose nuts had shells so tender and thin that a mere touch would leave the flesh naked. And then, planted in an enormous clay pot, grew his fructiferous tree of delicacies, the trunk of which split off into three boughs, one engrafted with pomegranates, one with golden pears, and the third with tinzenite-red oranges. And interspersed amongst his real trees he had bronze trees elaborately painted in impossible colours and along certain walks there were beds of artificial flowers made of ivory and electrum.

He collected dogs from Epirus, Dalmatia and Lacedaemon; introduced to the island goats from Scyros and Naxos, sheep from Miletus and Attica, and swine from Sicily. He had an aviary with diverse kinds of birds, including ospreys, and even a theocronus, a bird generated from a male hawk and a female eagle. There was a crane with two heads, a chicken with four wings . . .

XIV.

He was also a patron of letters and was the first to have the Homeric epics collated; and he collected a library of all known writers, a vast hall full of rare and valuable papyri from Egypt, Macedonia, Persia and beyond. There was the *Theogonia* of Cnossos, a *Historical Geography of the Aegean Sea* by Archilochos the Parian, *The Smyrnian Epic* of Mimnermus, and Colaios' *Calculation of the Length of the World by the Assistance of Oblique Triangles*. He had the complete works of Agias, Arctinus and Creophylus; he had books on harmony, warfare, rain water, indivisible lines, appellative nouns, lawgivers, definitions of neutral things, Zacynthian suppers, economics, asymmetric numbers, erotics, etymologies, mechanical problems, dialectic terms, votive offerings, hunting, and a great variety of other instructive subjects. And he let the architects, engineers and poets of his court have free access to these works, thus greatly advancing the level of the sciences of the island, so they did match or exceed in every way those of other parts of the world.

XV.

From a Catalogue of Literary Treasures:

PHILAMMON:
A HYMN TO DEMETER, engraved on a heart made of mountain copper

PEISANDER OF CAMIROS:
EPIC OF HERACLES, in forty books on amphitheatric papyrus

ARCTINUS OF MILETUS AND EUMELUS OF CORINTH:
TITANOMACHY

IMHOTEP:
ON QUADRILATERAL MASONRY, written in hieratic script with notes in an unknown hand in Greek

CINTHAETHON OF LACEDAEMON:
OEDIPODEA

LESCHES OF MITYLENE:
LITTLE ILIAD

EUGAMMON OF CYCENE:
TELEGONY, written in gold lettering on vellum of gazelle

HESIOD:
AEGIMIUS, with pictorial designs by Clitias and Ergotimos

ANTIMACHUS OF TEAS:
THE AFTER-BORN, decorated with bands of purple and black rays

ASIOS, SON OF AMPHIPTOLEMOS:
EPIC OF PHOINIX, written in boustrophedon, Greek cattle-track

HYBRIAS:
WINE SONGS, a series of eighteen, each engraved on an individual wax tablet

PANYASSIS OF HALICARNASSUS:
HERACLEIA, in the handwriting of the author

OLEN:

HYMNS

PHOCYLIDES:
EPIGRAMS AGAINST BESTIALITY, recto
STYPTIC SAYINGS, verso

XVI.

Fragment of a Popular Song Invented by Ibycus[1]
Sung to the Sound of that Instrument Called the Sam-
buca, also Invented by Ibycus:

You are always aloft, my mind,
Like some old porphyris, with outstretched
wings.

Said Ibycus:
Spartan girls are naked-thighed and man-
crazy.

---

1 Ibycus, the great poet and inventor of the victory ode, escaped from
the Greek city of Rhegium, in southern Italy, where he had been offered
dictatorship, but renounced such responsibility in favour of pursuing verse.
Hearing that the arts were flourishing in Samos, he travelled there and, upon
obtaining audience with Polycrates, recited that poem which begins with
the lines:

In the spring alone do the pomegranates and quinces grow,
in the sacred Virgins' Grove, furnished with water by brooks;
and swelling grapes prosper beneath the cool shade of vine-shoots;
but for me no season exists when love reclines in silence.

Said Anacreon:
I am pining for you boy with maiden's eyes
and voice more musical than a monaulos,
but you ignore me, oblivious to the fact that
you hold the reins of my heart.

Said Anacreon:
He's so fresh; he exhales sagda and his skin
smells like apples.

Said Anacreon:
Love, like a smith, hits with a huge hammer.

Said Anacreon:
In truth boy, you are more skittish than a
horse.

XVII.

Bathyllus was a youth of remarkable beauty, thoroughly
effeminate in his manners. His hair, saturated with
odiferous oil of flowers, was parted evenly in the middle
and streamed down over either cheek; he had a plump
neck, a delicate mouth and a full jaw with a dimpled
chin. His eyes were painted green with malachite, like
a woman's. He sang the song which begins with the
words:

Pallid and pink as his *****
was his penumbra;
blushing is my heart when aflame,

plucking at his lyre with his plectrum between each saccharine verse. When this was over all applauded vigorously. Polycrates, his face flushed with wine, offered a toast to the young man.

Ibycus murmured, "Bathyllus, off-shoot of the opal-eyed Graces and pet of the flaxen-haired Muses, it is you that Cypris and Persuasion of the tender looks rear amid the roses."

Anacreon, touching the young man's hand, declared it to be "softer than a fine robe," looking at his complexion, said that it was "fresher than water," at his neck, "whiter than milk or even an egg," <boiling me. harder. hotter than rock. fire. you filly look askance at me and think old me unskilled while well bridle you I would and turn you about the limits of the track . . . but now you feed in the meadow and lightly frisk, play, for you do not have a skilful rider experienced with young studs>.

"Bring me water—mixed with wine," the poet cried out to the pantry slave, "Instantly boy! And bring also,

Many flowers interwoven; I mean garlands;
Then fill my cup; and so elevated
Beneath the glad dominion of the vine
I might not think of hopeless love."
" . . . Auge . . ."

". . . A woman with thick ankles is a whore."

"The groans of Auge are far sweeter in tone than a harp."

"Very Anacreontic," said lushy Anacreon as his eyes followed a train of Sicilian slaves winding into the room laden with baskets heaped high with purple-hued apples from Corinth, Tithrasian figs and Carystian nuts; golden bowls filled with dainties, fish steeped in Cleonaean vinegar, pink shrimps swimming in saffron-coloured broth, fried daffodils, chickens glazed with honey and meat suffocated with caper sauce.

"My cook, Echoiax, when growing up," Polycrates said, "never played with hoops and balls as other children did, but with cloves of garlic and roasted giblets and even as a baby demanded that his mother's milk be boiled with Lampsacene honey before he would condescend to drink it."

Polycrates, ensconced in a pile of purple cushions, ate a plate of rape dressed with new wine and raisins, two roasted crabs and a good portion of batter-fried piglet raised on milk; cercope, monkey grasshoppers, to further stimulate the appetite; stuffed crayfish and an eel with green garlic sauce.

"Watch those twenty-four white beasts," said Heracles, standing on one leg, with one hand uplifted, himself outstretched in the posture of Hermes, "and watch the red one lick them all."

"He can certainly eat a great deal," Maeandrius commented.

"It is fine," Telesarchus, a citizen, said. "If he gets

sick he will vomit gold."

XVIII.

Polycrates, hearing of the glory Theodorus had given the Spartans, sent a letter recalling him to Samos with promises of great reward. The artist returned home and was given audience with the tyrant, who sat eating fruit and listening to his daughter, shallow-eyed long-necked Eriphyle, recite with stressed euphony the poems of Sappho: (*this dust was unmarried Timas . . . who when she perished, all her virgin friends groomed with sharpened steel their lovely curls, and to her tomb brought and strew those hairs*) . . . . . . That malleable and ductile, that precious yellow metallic element was hauled out, commissions piled one on top of the next: for statues, for temples, to re-build the Heraion in grand style . . . . A chest of coins from Lydia set in the middle of the room . . .

"Father," Eriphyle said (her own hair more gold than the gold, quince-coloured, dyed so with chrusoxylon, more commonly called Scythian wood), "it seems to me that you are moving far too quickly. It is true that we have heard marvellous things of this man; but here he is, at his first interview with you, his cup of wine barely tasted, and he has already received charges enough to last him more than a lifetime. Would it not be best if, before intrusting him with such a number of important tasks, before trusting such a quantity of precious metal into his hands, you tried his ability with some smaller project?"

"But daughter, I have seen his work in Delphi[1], and we all know what he has done for the Lacedaemonians."

"You have seen what he can do, or is reputed to have done, in foreign parts, but we do not yet know what he can do in Samos."

"Well . . ." said Polycrates.

Theodorus bowed to the king, more gracefully still to Eriphyle, and then, plucking a single coin from the treasure, said: "Allow me to borrow this for a short time, to give you some slight demonstration of my skill." He drained his wine and took his leave and three days later returned.

To Eriphyle he presented a golden fly, in exact proportions and likeness to the real insect. To Polycrates, a ring of sardonyx set in gold, a ring of truly marvellous workmanship and unsurpassed beauty, its band intertwined vine tendrils across which satyrs leaped lightly forth and played on pipes of reeds, and its gem

---

1   For Croesus, that absurdly wealthy king and client (adorned with olivine, sparkling diamonds, dewy-golden heliodor, dyed raiment—everything extravagant, considered attractive—his person presenting a fantastically imposing, seriously stunning vision—him who first, with refining furnace and hearth, turned alluvial gold into its component parts of silver and gold, him the first to strike coins of solid silver and gold, to surpass simple electrum, to initiate the bimetallic system of coinage) who wanted something magnificent to give to the Delphians, Theodorus made two bowls, one of silver and one of gold, each able to hold five-thousand and one-hundred gallons of liquid, which were to be used as mixing-bowls at the feast of the Divine Appearance. They were marvellously chased, their surfaces embossed with numerous picturesque sequences . . .

engraved with a lyre seal.

Theodorus, together with his father Roicos, under the patronage of Polycrates, invented a spectacular method of ore smelting and hollow casting. On his own he invented the water level, the lock and key, the lathe, the carpenter's rule and square; and through these tools was able to greatly advance his art. . . . . . . He cast a statue of Polydor which was installed in the temple of Ares and then, at a later date, a statue of Polycrates' cook, Echoiax, in the attitude of a valiant warrior, wielding pot and ladle, which was sent as an offering to Delphi. He also cast a miniature of himself in bronze, a perfect likeness; in his right hand he held a file, while on the extended fingers of his left sat a chariot drawn by four horses, a masterpiece of chasing, so small that the very fly that he made would have been able to cover it with its wings. . . . . . . Then later, he made a golden vine with grapes of purple sapphires for Pythios, the son of Atys and grandson of Croesus, which that famous extravagant gave to Darius[2] . . .

. . . . . . in Ephesus he built a system of central heating into the Temple of Diana; and on Samos, together with his father, he rebuilt the Heraion, constructed the greatest temple in the world, with one-hundred and twenty-three large columns in the circular court and ten in the great open entrance hall.

. . . . . . The sacred road leading to the Heraion Poly-

---

2   <<Ezra 4:5-24, 5:5-7, 6:1-15; Neh. 12:22; Dan. 5:31, 6:1-28, 9:1, 11:1; Hag. 1:1-15, 2:10; Zech. 1:1-7, 7:1; 1 Esdr. 2:30, 3:1-8, 4:47, 5:2-6, 5:73, 6:1-34, 7:1-5; 1 Mac. 1:1, 12:7>>

crates had paved with stones and lined with monu-
ments, temples and statues; four broad-shouldered
youths by the sculptor Geneleos[1], each fifteen feet high;
in front of the temple was seated Aeaces in marble and
two statues in wood of Amasis, which that king had
sent by boat all the way from Egypt. Also on the road
was the tomb of Radine and Leontichos, where all those
jilted in their sentiments would go to pray, and this he
had embellished . . . . . . Then there were the . . . Panai-
mon, Proastion . . . Apollon Pythaeus, built by Mnesar-
chos, the father of Pythagoras, designed by Theodorus
who also, together with his brother, carved the statue of
the god, Telecles signing the right foot, Theodorus the
left. . . . . . . Demeter Enelcyses . . . and the temple of
Hermes Charetodotus, during whose name-day it was
allowed for all Samians to steal . . . . the city decorated to profusion with flowers, those diverse blooms
Samos was famous for, lateritious crocus all the way to
yellow; orchids, cliff rose, hyacinth, white water lily,
dark red tulip and three-coloured chamomile; amaryl-
lis and soft narcissus fed on dew; haymeadows and sea
daffodil; tiny pink-flowered and long-stalked cyclamen
called Chelonion with its tubers shaped like turtles; lily
and rose-chalice and moist anemone, and dark-glowing
violet; liontooth and ox-eye . . . . Tauropoleion .
. . . .

    . . . the Bouleuterion, an assembly hall . . . .

---

1   "Look at the foolish smiles on their faces," said Theodorus; "the smiles
of idiots or boys made stupid by love. . . . Truly, even Polymedes of Argos
deserves more praise than Geneleos."

theatre . . . . . . the people of Samos dedicated a gymnasium to Eros and called the festival held in his honour
the Eleutheria. . . . . . . And, in order to counteract the
tendencies of the youth, distract their minds away from
their male companions, he had constructed an area
in the middle of the city which he called the Laura,
a place meant to compete in splendid dissipation with
the Ancon of Sardis, and in it he let be established many
houses of prostitution, restaurants and food stands
which sold victuals calculated to gratify intemperance
and promote enjoyment, and other shops where every
apparatus of luxury was sold; pavonine garments . . .
golden ornaments and silver footed stools . . . female
flutists and harpers played in the street from daybreak
. . . and in numerous companies the young men and
old would pace lazily along, their hair dripping with
sweet smelling oil, bodies richly clad in long and soft
purple garments, those garments usually reserved only
for kings and which were worth eight times their weight
in silver . . . and spent their time at dice, filling their
bellies with meat, drinking Chian wine in Spartan cups,
and singing loose songs to the music of the noisy ennea-
chord . . .

XIX.

Contents of Eriphyle's dressing case:

Item: Excrementa of Egyptian crocodiles, for the complexion
Item: Oesipum, for embellishing and cleaning the complexion
Item: A comb made of Libyan ivory
Item: Ointment of orris
Item: A depilatory ointment, made from the boiled and crushed bones of a spoonbill, mixed with fly dung, oil of ben, sycamore juice, storax gum, and cucumber
Item: A perfume of crocus-oil
Item: Bdellium

XX.

Epistle:

Amasis, King of Egypt to Polycrates, Lord of the Sea, *Prosperity*
I feel it likely that this letter will reach you in both good health and spirits, as you are the most fortunate of men, one who suffers not from some regrettable malady of

the joints but from great opulence. Every activity you undertake terminates in success and it seems to many that your destiny is not to be simply Lord of the Sea, but to be lord of all of Ionia and Greece.

The normal reaction of a man, when he hears of the success of a friend and ally, is to feel great joy, as all like to know that those who are close to their hearts are doing well. Yet, dear Polycrates, your excessive prosperity does not cause me joy, but the contrary emotion, because I am quite certain that it must fill even deities such as Horus and Isis with discontent and jealousy, if I may make so bold a statement.

For long now have I, fulfilling my duty as a king, studied the principles of signs and portents, livanomancy, extispicy and halomancy, have steered my own course in life by the entrails of fish, the mode in which cocks peck at grains of millet and the particulars of wine when poured on the naked flesh of a virgin's back, and thus flatter myself that I know a little something on the subject. So now I tell you this in plain words: if this great success of yours is not sometimes given intermission, you will be pitched into disaster; for never in the history of the world has there been a man who, after having all his enterprises terminate as he desired, did not ultimately experience catastrophe and whose story did not end in tragedy.

Now, according to me there is only one way to avoid this change of fortune: reflect and decide which of all your treasures you consider to be the finest, which you hold most dear, which would give you the most pain to have taken from you. Then, no matter what that article might be, take it and dispose of it so that it will never again be seen by human eyes or touched by human hands. This is my advice.

Polycrates ran his fingers through his beard, touched his lips to the signet ring made by Theodorus, and knew. The next day he went out to sea in one of his ships and, when he was well into deep water, took the ring from his finger and cast it far from him. That night, back at his palace, he wept and pulled a handful of hairs from his beard; for throwing the ring away had been like fratricide, only he felt greater sorrow now than he had when he had murdered his brother, because at that time he had gained a kingdom, while now the only thing he had to show for his action was a naked finger.

"But you should feel happy," suggested Ibycus, "since, as you believe, by this action you have staved off the jealousy of the gods."

"Have I; or have I simply been prey to the jealousy of Amasis? I have always propitiated the gods, and they have always favoured me. And, after all, it was not them who suggested I do myself harm."

XXI.

Cold-eyed, lank-haired Maeandrius, son of Maeandrius, brother of Lycaretus and sneak-thief Charilaus, was intelligent, of a thin, unmuscular form, well versed in the basics of flattery, clear-headed and of the supple morals suitable to one who wishes to please his master. The oily accents of his voice were glossed with silver. He was subservient to his betters, bold with his equals and contemptuous of those of lower position.

"A man wishes to see you," Maeandrius said. "He is at the gate and insists."

"Does he appear to be in a violent state of mind?"

"On the contrary, he seems to be quite well disposed."

With Polycrates' consent, a fisherman was shown into the chamber, followed by four stout lads bearing an enormous epinephelus on a stretcher.

"My lord," said the fisherman with an awkward bow, "this morning I offered my usual crust of bread and drop of wine to Artemis of the Fishing-Nets, and today she has been good to me, letting me win this trophy of the sea. Though I know I could sell it for an attractive sum to some rich man or to one of the better eateries in the Laura, I have refrained from such a temptation, and have carried it here instead, as a gift to you Poly-crates,—for it is a fish worthy of your magnitude."

Polycrates, lover of cold-blooded aquatic verte-brates, thanked the fisherman, promised him a gift of a Sardian net, and dismissed him . . . an invitation to return that evening for supper . . . . . . good fortune could not be thrown off and *<epinephelus. brought from anticamera of the abyss. properly prepared as sweet to the palate as some pretty nulipara. or effemi-nate . . . > . . .*

. . . Under the supervision of Maeandrius the fish was ported back to the kitchen, where it fell into the hands of Echoiax, that most sublime culinary master who, standing behind piles of coriander and cinnamon, blushed when he saw it, wondering at once how he should cook it, what sort of sauce he should prepare, whether gold or green, or with turnsole sauce azure, to make it as if still swimming in the deep sea—or then again, maybe simply tucked into a great bed of well-turbaned mushrooms.

"Whatever you do," said Maeandrius in a haughty voice, "make sure that you do not over-cook it or over-power its own natural flavour with some foreign addi-tive."

"These critics are like eunuchs," Echoiax mur-mured. "They know what to do but they can't do it."

So thinking, the cook slit open the belly of the fish and, while removing its guts, found a precious piece of jewellery, a ring of marvellous workmanship and unsur-passed beauty; and this was soon restored to Polycrates,

Echoiax chattering away about the marvel of the fish.

Fragments of an Epistle:

Pol[ycrates to A]masis,

      . . . . . . so that is how it happened . . .
      . . . more than a touch providential . . .
. . .

Fragments of an Epistle:

[Amasis] to Polycrates,

      . . . . . . beyond our control . . . . . . that
which inescapably befalls one . . . agency . .
. the order of things . . . .
    So be it. I hereby dissolve our friend-
ship. Disaster will surely come to you, and
when it does, I do not want to grieve.

Polycrates was enraged when he read this letter.
"The man says that, in order not to grieve for my mis-
fortune, one that he proclaims himself the augur of, he
would rather not be my friend. Well—he who repulses
the friendship of Polycrates contracts a hard enemy."

XXII.

Maeandrius caught sight of Eriphyle strolling amongst the feathery-branched tamarisks, wearing nothing but a cimbericon, a short and transparent frock.

"Enjoying the weather?" he asked, approaching.

"Enjoying being alone," she said in glacial tones.

"But companionship can often be very entertaining."

"So you are offering to entertain?"

"It is lonely here; I am at your service."

"I believe that you have a filthy mind."

"Do you think I am over-ambitious?"

"I have no idea about the state of your ambition."

"I am a man."

"You are disgusting. Let go of my hand, or I will tell my father and he will have you thrown into the sea."

She turned and walked away. Maeandrius felt the anger of inadequacy; his attraction was left to rot and turn to hate; on Samos that day a pig was born that looked just like an elephant, except for its feet, which were conventional.

XXIII.

Polydor, in charge of a patrol of nine pentecosters,

waylaid in the Sea of Crete a ship bound from Egypt to Lacedaemon, a ship sent by King Amasis to the Spartans with gifts. The Samian marshal attacked and robbed it of its cargo; five dozen psicters of pickled gourd, as many amphorae of Teniotic barley-wine, a portrait of the king, a good deal of silver plate, two bridles of gold, headtires of linen and a corselet of finely-textured linen and gold with numerous figures of asps, rams and women with the spotted bodies of leopards and lotuses for tails woven into its fabric. Polycrates, when he saw the splendour of this latter prize, laughed and ridiculed the name of Amasis, that king who had forfeited his friendship.

XXIV.

The bronze statue Telecles made of Bathyllus, which was placed in the Heraion, was roundly abused by Geneleos, not only to private individuals, but in public places and in a voice loud and calculated to draw attention . . . . . .

"And look at your own work," said Telecles, "stiff and lifeless, stacked alongside the road like so many upright corpses."

. . . Words, phonological shapes, changed to rough and injurious physical force . . . . . .

. . . . . . Telecles . . . struck by Geneleos with a hammer . . .

. . . . . . Theodorus buried his brother and carved a small monument for him with an inscription authored by Ibycus which read:

Here lies Telecles, who carved in stone and cast in bronze,
And left behind a name more enduring than either.

. . . . . . Theodorus watched Geneleos, the man's thick thighs rubbing against each other as he walked through a field sprinkled white with crocus, and then into a cypress grove . . . . . . called his name and, when he turned, struck out with a dagger, but Geneleos pulled back, the blade merely grazed his arm, and he then turned and ran, up the hill and through the stately firs, to the bare summit. . . . . . . Geneleos picked up a large stone and turned upon his assailant, ready to defend himself as best he could. But then his look of aggressive fear turned to one of astonishment and he stood frozen in his tracks so that when Theodorus stabbed him in the head, he made hardly a move, his gaze fixed out to sea. And so Theodorus now turned, and looked. The sea, a delicious harebell blue under the post meridian sun, was incrusted with Spartan ships of war; and Geneleos rested dead at his feet.

XXV.

Cambyses, that son of Cyrus[1] and King of Persia, fratricide and incestuous sororicide . . . gathering an armament, preparing for war with Egypt, against Amasis . . . . . . Cambyses, knowing that Amasis was in bad odour with Polycrates, sent an envoy to the latter to ask for naval assistance. Polycrates rounded up those Samians whom he had least faith in, possible political opponents, those who he thought had the potential to stir revolt, sent them in forty ships to Egypt as food for sharp-fanged javelins and arrows . . . but off Carpathus the crews, led by Sarapammon, revolted. They chopped their Persian captains into fine bits, fed them to the sea fowls, and sailed back to Samos, hoping to cause an insurrection. Polycrates set out what portions he could of his own fleet and suffered substantial losses, but with volleys of arrows fired into the sea was able to keep the rebels from landing, and so these latter fled to Lacedaemon.

---

1   <<2 Chr. 36:22-23; Ezra 1:1-8, 3:7, 4:3-5, 5:13-17, 6:3-14; Isa. 44:28, 45:1; Dan. 1:21, 6:28, 10:1; 1 Esdr. 2:1-11, 4:44-57, 5:55-73, 6:17-25, 7:4; Bel. 1>>

XXVI.

The Spartans lived in a way far different from the Samians; their babies, if born weak or deformed, were taken to the Apothetae, a chasm, where they were left to die; the strong were bathed, tempered in wine. The Lacedaemonians ate in phiditiae, common halls, and lived in barracks, the women separated from the men, and in the winter they went without shoes and slept without blankets. The houses they lived in were rough and made from logs. . . . . . . Their women, on the wedding night, would be dressed as men and have their hair clipped off, so opposed were those people to all forms of effeminacy. Perfume and dyed clothing were both illegal . . . . . . spent their time in military training . . . . . .

. . . . . those laconic sayings of the Lacedaemonians . . . . . .

. . . . . ."Know yourself," said Chilon . . .

. . . "Do tomorrow's work today."

. . . A Spartan, being asked by a loquacious man, "Who is the greatest Spartan?" replied, "He who is least like you."

. . . . . . "Everything in moderation," said Chilon . . .

XXVII.

When the renegade Samians reached Sparta, they were given an audience with the euphors and the diarchic kings, Anaxandridas and Ariston[1]. Sarapammon talked at great length, doused the kings with flowery compliments, set off the fireworks of his elocution before the assembly; with an excellent choice of language, with a calculatedly-trembling voice complained of Polycrates, pointed out that the man was not only a problem for him and his associates, but had also disrespected Sparta, had stolen the magnificent bronze vase which they had years earlier intended for King Croesus and more recently stolen a boat-load of goodies that the Egyptian King Amasis had intended for them, "and," he concluded, "the Samians themselves are a repressed people and will rebel, gladly overthrow their tyrant and afterwards be immensely grateful to you Lacedaemonians."

Sarapammon stood now silent in the middle of the room, arms akimbo, triumphant. The Spartans looked at each other in amazement. No one could by effort of memory recall the first half of the speech and, as to the second, not a man there had been able to follow its circumlocutionary logic.

The next day the Samians returned. Sarapammon

---

1 The same man who married the most unattractive Virgin in Laconia, but Helen made her the most beautiful. At the gate of Ariston's house was the tomb of the great hero Astrabacos, who had been driven mad by Artemis. The dead man slept with Ariston's wife, two months before the latter actually married her, and impregnated the lady with Demaratos.

lifted up an empty sack which he had brought with him, turned it upside down and shook it. "The sack needs flour," he said.

"Needs flour," said Anaxandridas.

"The sack!" cried Sarapammon.

Ariston: "Two words . . ."

Anaxandridas: ". . . too many."

Sarapammon: "Help?"

The kings: "Yes."

Then Sarapammon declared that time should not be wasted, but they should set out straight away and take Samos by surprise, for, he said, "A fish's strength lies in its tail; Polycrates' strength lies in his navy."

XXVIII.

Knots of youths were seen on the street corners, some whose cheeks were livid with fear, whispering. . . . The Spartans were notorious warriors, and few men like to be drained of their blood. . . . Polycrates met with his aides, with Polydor, Periphoretus Artemon and Maeandrius, and discussed strategy.

"We have no time to properly man our ships," Polydor said. "It will be as much as we can do to put half a dozen into action."

Polycrates: "They would easily be overcome, then the Spartans would take the harbour, setting fire to the rest or capturing them."

Artemon: "Take those half dozen ships and this minute have them laden with stones and put in a line to block the harbour."

An action done; and then, to inspire his soldiers and mercenaries with enthusiasm, Polycrates offered a reward of three staters for every Spartan or renegade killed in the ensuing battle; to deter betrayal amongst his own subjects, he shut up their wives and children in the sheds built to shelter his ships, and was ready to burn them in case of need.

XXIX.

The Lacedaemonians, led by Ariston, arrived before Samos—with their fire-bearing priest who carried the lamp lighted at the shrine of wolfish Zeus;—with seventy-eight warships, each full of men in sparkling helmets and cuirasses, wielding immense spears and many armed with bows. They pulled their ships sternward up on the beach below the Poseidium and, after sacrificing the customary she-goat, proceeded to lay siege to the city. Under the direction of a certain Membliaros, ladders were built; and while Polycrates was behind the walls saying words befitting the occasion to his own people, the Spartans, one to the next, spoke their minds:

"We have a reputation of winning battles . . ."

". . . not losing them."

"It would be absurd to fail in this land attack . . ."

" . . . against a people who are only expert in sea warfare and banqueting."

The soldiers banged their spears against their shields; the flutists struck up a tune of war and the men sang in deep bass voices that marching song of Tyrtaios that begins with the lines:

> With a wound in his chest where the spear
> he was facing pierced
> that massive guard of his shield, and went
> through his breastplate as well . . .

A crack corps of brave individuals, pioneers, now rushed upon the walls, carrying the ladders amongst them. They scrambled over the dangerous palisades; some were shot with arrows and killed; others bravely bridged the moat, only to find that, when the ladders they had hauled forward at such great risk were leaned against that tall and vertical solid structure of stone, each and every one of them was too short; and so the men retreated, cheeks hot with shame, darts flying at their heels. This threw the main body of soldiers into confusion and they broke rank. Polycrates, seeing this, sent out a band of his Thracian peltasts to harass them, and a number of the enemy were slain.

The next day Ariston had Membliaros executed and, under his own supervision, had battering rams and fresh ladders built.

Then, the following day, at dawn, Ariston spoke

to his men. "The Samians," he said, "spend not only their nights but even their days relaxing on cushions of down, while if we rest at all, it is on shields and breastplates. They dine on turtles fattened on millet seed and suffocated in sauce, drink unmixed wine from gold and silver cups, their foreheads wreathed in mint, while we eat daggers and drink dripping torches, our brows crowned with catapults. Can we Spartans not overcome such men, can we return home in utter disgrace?"

The flutists struck up, and the soldiers marched forward without gap in their line of battle, the men singing in deep bass voices that song of Tyrtaios that begins with the lines:

> An old warrior whose head is white
> and beard grey, exhaling his vigorous soul
> into the dust, clutching his bloody genitals
> in his hands . . .

. . . . . . The Samians poured down upon the assailants burning pitch mixed with resin and sulphur, difficult to extinguish naphtha, as well as great stones, many weighing as much as three-hundred pounds, and these would sweep the Spartans off their ladders, and when well-aimed knock the heads off of the battering-rams, and then sometimes they were able to break them off with the aid of nooses, or deaden their blows with baskets of wool suspended by ropes. They extinguished the Spartans' fire-bearing missiles with water and vinegar, and deleted the force of others by means of sheets of linen held loosely above the ramparts. And all these tricks were thought up by Artemon, who had his servants carry him about in a hammock, close to the ground in case he should fall out, and with a shield over him as protection from any descending object.

Yet still many flaming arrows found their mark, and several buildings caught fire, some roofs caved in, and some inhabitants were crushed under blazing beams. Fathers covered their faces with their hands, so as not to see the charred and mangled corpses of their sons. Some men wept silently in corners while others screamed in rage. The archers were put upon the walls and let their arrows fly. Amotion, a huge and great Lacedaemonian warrior, had an arrow enter his mouth, piercing his pharynx and descending straight back to his spine, and he drank his last draft, swallowed his own blood as his soul said farewell to his body. Another Spartan, Oiolycos by name, felt an arrow enter just below his left hip, and shrugged his shoulders only to find a second fly through his wrist, a third clang menacingly against his helmet, a half dozen more hurry by, whistling oblivion. Some men dragged their wounded comrades from the field, others went gladly forward, as if to meet their lovers, with gore-flecked thighs, stepping through that field enveloped in the dark cloud of death. A group of Sarapammon's rebels advanced upon the wall under the cover of blindages. One for a moment lifted his head above the guard, and fell a cadaver.

Silhouettes of men, singularly and in groups, cries of rage and terror, the shrill sound of arrows, fumes,

stench of burning flesh. . . . Each day the dead grew more
numerous, particularly among the Spartans, the lives
of many lovely youths lost in the uneven blur of war.
Two of the city gates were beaten in. But the breaches
that were made during the hours from sunrise to sunset
were repaired during the hours from sunset to sunrise.
The walls of Samos seemed impenetrable; their ditches
like gaping mouths with an insatiable thirst for blood.
. . . The attackers became actually desperate for victory. . . . In one of the assaults upon the walls, by sheer
will and suffering heavy losses, they forced their way
to the top of the tower which stood by the sea on the
side of the city where the arsenal was. Polycrates saw
the peril, and with a band of light infantry went to the
place and proceeded to beat back the assailants. Mean-
while, at the upper tower, which stood on the ridge of
the hill, the besieged, both mercenaries and Samians,
opened the gates and made a counter attack; but after
they had killed a number of the enemy and captured
seventeen of their shields, they turned back. The Lacedaemonians, pushing after them with their long spears,
slew numbers; and two Spartans, Archias and Lycopes,
actually managed to enter the walls, but their retreat
was cut off from behind, and so they died, and later,
their bravery being much admired by the Samians,
they were buried at public expense, with great honour.

XXX.

"We will never take the city by storm."

"So we will defer our ambitions."

"But will we gratify them?"

"Yes. We will starve the Samians out."

Polycrates sent off Polydor, who left the city through the tunnel of Eupalinus, hiked over the hills and swam from Samos to Ephesus, where a number of Samian crafts were kept. These, under his command, set off and patrolled the waters, interceding and harassing any supply ship sent to the Spartans. The Spartans sent out their foraging parties of Helots to gather food, but these were continually pursued by small groups of Polycrates' javelin-bearing Naxians and so were in no way able to take in enough supplies to satisfy the hunger of the substantial number of men encamped on the island. Democedes, that most brilliant of pharmacists, made pellets of tithymal and bean meal and these were clandestinely scattered in the water all around the island, and they thus killed all the fish in the surrounding ocean, making it barren of meat, and those fish that floated to the surface of the water or washed ashore were foul and poisoned.

Echoiax, in the open air of public spaces, roasted lambs, calves and kids on spits, dressed the meat with rich gravy and served it up with sweet bread while the holy singers of Hera joined their voices together and let them melodiously drift on the wind, together with the perfume of succulent flesh, toward the enemy camps. The Spartans listened with their noses more than their ears; some Samian renegades wept to hear the songs they well knew while excluded from all native celebration.

"Surrender," Ariston shouted from below the walls.

"Spartan, you came here and compelled us to take up arms. Now we don't want to lay them down."

"We will starve you out!"

"Starve us out!" laughed Polycrates. "Why look here man . . ." And so saying he had two citizens hurl a well-fatted pig over the ramparts. A duo of hungry renegades ran forward and secured the broken, squealing creature while those behind the walls looked on with broad grins and laughter. Samian warriors held loaves of bread in their hands and stuffed their mouths full; a group of Illyrian mercenaries merrily shared out some cheese-cakes, while a Sythic bowman, wearing a peaked felt cap of almost absurd length, waved a great joint of meat as if it were a flag.

Ariston's chin sunk to his breast. Truly it was a shame, the besiegers starving and not the besieged!

And so, after forty days the Spartans retreated, took their ships and left; at home ridiculed by the women who would have rather seen none come back alive at all, who would have rather paraded weeping through the streets while banging on brass pots, than see such numbers return in disgrace.

. . . And Sarapammon and his rebels went off, caused

trouble in other parts of Greece.

XXXI.

Said Pythagoras:

The square of the hypotenuse of a right triangle is equal to the sum of the squares of the other two sides.

Graffito, in Eupalinus's tunnel:

By the Delphian god! Right here Crimon had fun with Pharnabazus, slave of eximious Hipponicus.

Graffito; reckoning on the wall of an inn:

1st bread 8, wine 2, dates 1
2nd bread 8, wine 2, fish 2
3rd lentils 2, wine 2, cheese 2
4th cheese 1, bread 8, oil 3, wine 3
5th bread 8, oil 5, bowl 1, bread for the slave 2, wine 2
6th wine for the winner 1, bread 8, wine 2, gosling 5
7th bread 2, for women 8, wheat 1, cucumber 1, incense 1, cheese 2, sausage 1, oil 7

Said Pythagoras:

Aphrodite as an evening star is the same as Aphrodite as a morning star.

Graffito, in the barracks of the peltasts:

Brimias the Thracian makes the girls sing.

Said Ibycus:[1]

---

1 . . . the Isthmian games, in Corinth, with chariot races and competitions
in poetry and music; and so Ibycus set out from Samos by ship, debarked at
Megara, and from there made his way on foot, as far as the sacred grove of
Poseidon, reciting,

Myrtle-berries with violets mixed,
And helichryse and apple blossoms,
And roses, and the tender daphne.

He looked toward the west, toward the Acrocorinthos rising in isolated grandeur above the nearer and lesser heights of the countryside; toward the east,
toward the amazingly blue waters of the Saronic Gulf; a flock of cranes flew
overhead. "All hail you friendly squadron," Ibycus shouted, "companions
from across the sea,—we both come from far in search of kindly reception!"
In juxtaposition to his words, two robbers, hairy-armed Brotachus and cruel
Timotheus, at that moment revealed themselves. Brotachus struck down
Ibycus with a crude club; as he fell, the latter's eyes flashed toward the sky;
he called out, "Revenge me!" Timotheus, with a sharp blade, slit the poet's
throat, submerged him in purple death. . . . Later the body was found and
recognised by a Corinthian who knew him. And the people, hearing of this
crime, gathered around and the tribunal and demanded that the criminals
be caught—but there was no evidence; the magistrates could do nothing.
. . . That night a black bull, with gilded horns and hooves and garlands
around his neck, was brought to the Palaimonion and sacrificed, burned
whole. The next day came the competition for which Ibycus had travelled.
And the amphitheatre was full. The choristers sang; the poets, Hipponax,
Xenophanes and demonstrative Thespis, to mention a few, came and recited
verses—each one dedicating their words to fallen Ibycus, and each trying
to outdo the next in pathetic lamentation. Then Simonides, with sorrowful
countenance, walked forward and in elegiac metre denounced the criminals and described the miseries they would suffer, if not in this life, then in
the next; and his final words were a plea for whoever knew of the crime to
denounce the murderers. And all were terrified to hear of the poetic fate of
the cold-blooded killers, not least the killers themselves who sat a mere ten
rows back, clutching the hems of their robes, where the gold staters they had
robbed were wrapped. And then, over the amphitheatre flew ever so slowly
that flock of cranes, and every head turned upward; and the birds cried
out. One of the murderers shot up from his seat, "Don't listen to them,"

The gods give much prosperity to those whom they wish to have it, but for the others they destroy it by the plans of the Moirae.

Graffito, on a boulder near the Proastion:

Barbax here danced cordax with Crimon; and melted.

XXXII.

Democedes: I saw Bathyllus in the Laura with Anacreon. And Anacreon was feeding him oysters.

<heart to wax. Bathyllus blazing sun>

Polycrates, sick with jealousy, had the hair of Bathyllus shorn from his head. . . . . . . Then he set fire to the gymnasium.

XXXIII.

There is something especially horrible about the unnatural decay of a handsome man. Polycrates had

---

he screamed. "They blame Timotheus and I for the murder, but they lie!" And so the murderer brought attention to himself and his companion. Their persons and homes were searched and property of Ibycus discovered. When carbon was ignited on the head of a long-eared ass and the criminals names recited, a crackling sound was heard, and so the two were put to death.

for years now over-indulged himself, with wine, often unmixed, rich foods, and numerous illicit relations with various specimens of the two sexes. No longer did he subject himself to the rigorous physical drills of his youth. As far as literature went, he turned from all serious study and began to peruse only the works of the lighter poets, those whose works dealt primarily with love and drink. He now had a decidedly gone-to-seed appearance, made all the more tragic by the fact that he tried to cover his flaws of feature with makeup and disguise. Numerous fine wrinkles surrounded his eyes, which themselves had taken on a glazed look, like those of a not particularly fresh fish. Every morning he applied a paste of Solomon's seal to his skin in order to keep these wrinkles at bay; this having failed, he applied to Democedes, who gave him an unguent of gum of frankincense, fresh moringa oil and cyperus grass. The hair of his head and beard, though still luxuriant, had turned grey and he died it with a decoction made from the rinds of the roots of the halm tree and the boiled blood of a black ox. His belly had grown large with fat and around his house and gardens he wore a long loose gown, violet-coloured and embroidered with figures of peacocks. When he went out he secured his belly and buttocks in a tight girdle and dressed in a turban of gold brocade and the soft purple robe of a king. He often found himself weak in the sports of Aphrodite and so had recourse to wine spiced with clary, to membrane of bitch, or cocks' stones fried with garlic.

XXXIV.

"I had a dream last night," Eriphyle said to her father one morning while they were breakfasting on poppy seed cakes and daffodil flowers steeped in honey of Hymettus. "I saw you raised up on some prominent place. . . . You were being laved and anointed by the hands of Zeus and the Sun."

Polycrates smiled. "Well," he said, "such a dream can only mean good things; surely it is the foretelling of a rich and happy future."

"Surely it is."

And they ate; and they licked the honey from their fingertips.

And during that time, other things occurred. A meteor darted from south to east. Lightning came from the clear sky, some citizens were struck, killed by bolts, as was a horse; one bolt struck the statue of Apollo that was placed near the theatre, and then again other statues, those of Demeter and Poseidon on horseback, began to sweat. There was an earthquake; subterranean groans were heard; bees swarmed about the temple of Dionysus and a profusion of owls were seen about the temple of Hermes; dogs prowled and whined through the city streets; a farmer dug up a jar of human flesh; blood flowed from beneath a bakeshop toward the Heraion and clods of earth mixed with bile were seen flying through the air.

XXXV.

". . . The herald is in the anti-chamber, waiting."

"What were the lines again?" said Polycrates to Anacreon, meek old lover of shorn Bathyllus. "What lust has now enslaved your mind . . ."

"What lust has now enslaved your mind," said Anacreon, "to wish to dance to amorous half-bored flutes."

"The herald is in the anti-chamber," repeated Maeandrius. "From Oroetes, Satrap of Sardis."

"Oroetes . . ." murmured Polycrates from his nest of purple cushions.

"I will send him in," said Maeandrius, and turned and walked briskly away.

A few moments later the herald was shown in. . . . He spoke, in low and respectful tones . . . of his master, Oroetes, Satrap of Phrygia, Satrap of Sardis . . . of a certain quarrel that had developed between his master and Mitrobates, Satrap of Dascyleium . . . of certain fears his master had concerning Cambyses. . . .

But Polycrates seemed not to listen. He did not even bother to look at the man, but instead lay half-inert, facing the wall and tracing with his big toe the patterns on one of his cushions. In the middle of the messenger's speech, Polycrates cut him off by addressing a question to Anacreon[1]. So he left, not only having failed to

---

1   Engraved on Anacreon's tomb:

elicit a reply to the questions Oroetes had given him to deliver, but having failed even to have his presence acknowledged by the Samian king.

When the herald returned to Oroetes and informed him of his treatment at the court of Polycrates, the satrap was very angry. He felt sickened by the fact that the neighbouring king held him in such low regard and determined to revenge the insult to his vanity. He sent a Lydian named Myrtus, the son of Gyges, and one of the most elegant men of the time, with another message to Polycrates stating that, due to certain unfortunate mis-understandings, he now had reason to fear for his life at the hands of Cambyses, King of Persia. Therefore, Oro-etes said, he would like to defect to Samos with all his treasure, which consisted of eight chests full of gold, of which he would give Polycrates half, if only the Samian king would come to Sardis in person to, "fetch me and give me protection".

At that time, Polycrates was in need of money. To keep a navy and large body of mercenaries, to keep so many artists and poets about his court, was no small expense—not to mention his own personal needs; and he was still ambitious for conquests.

"I would take him up on his offer, if I knew it was genuine, if I knew he had the gold."

"Let me then go to Oroetes," said Maeandrius, "and inspect the situation."

You stranger, who now stands before the tomb of Anacreon,
spill libation over me before departing; for I am a drinker of wine.

So the secretary went to Sardis and when he returned informed Polycrates that the satrap had shown him six chests full of bright lion-headed staters and two full of ingots of pale gold. "Oroetes is sincere in his offer," he said.

"And I am sincere in my desire to relieve him of his treasure," Polycrates said.

Tellias the Elean soothsayer sacrificed victims, but the livers of each were covered with hair. When he tried his hand at ovomancy, the egg white was in the shape of a hammer. He undertook divination by figs, by driftwood and by the coagulation of cheese, but each time with equally unpromising results. Yet, for all this, Polycrates in no way changed his plans and had his red-cheeked pentecoster readied for the voyage.

The day of his departure was absolutely cloudless; and the sea was so calm that it seemed almost asleep. Eriphyle ran to the harbour in distress.

"Oroetes is a liar," she said to her father.

"And Maeandrius, son of Maeandrius?"

"A fool."

"And me?"

"My father."

"Go home, or I will have you married to dwarf Heracles!"

"At least he will not go bald as many other men do," Eriphyle jested and then smiled sadly.

Polycrates kissed her on the forehead and boarded the ship. His party consisted of a bodyguard of fifty picked men, Democedes the physician and Tellias the soothsayer who, as the boat glided over the sea, claimed that he saw in the formations of certain schools of fish inauspicious signs—but Polycrates, distracted by thoughts of fresh treasure, impelled by the will of the gods, still did not regard his words. The ship docked in Phocaea, and the party then made its way overland toward Sardis. On the way, however, they were ambushed by Oroetes and that man's one-thousand Persian bodyguards. Polycrates was bound, spit upon and taken to Colophon where he was tied to the tail-end of a cart and whipped all the way to Priene. Then he was dragged up to the summit of Mt. Mycale, to an open and conspicuous spot; raised up on a cross of pine, crucified with his front facing Samos, which he could actually see. Though exhausted and suffering great pain, he conducted himself with fortitude, even when the stakes were driven through his hands and feet, and joked in a feeble voice that he thought it a shame that he would now no longer be able to play the magdis to his Lacedaemonian hound; with rain he was washed by Zeus and, when the dew of agony came upon his skin, anointed by the fingers of the sun.

Eriphyle came to plead for her father. She offered ransom, not of mere money, but of whole islands and districts rich and fertile, but cruel Oroetes, drunk with fleeting power and advised to ruthless acts by Maeandrius, would not listen. In front of her he had Polycrates' intestines torn out and burned before the man's eyes; and she screamed in horror while her father was dumbfounded by agony, his soul, that self-moving number, seeping into the underworld. Oroetes had the young woman seized, personally robbed her of her virginity, then prostituted her in the public roads; and later, when she had been steeped in humiliation, he had her tortured, slivers of glass thrust under the nails of her fingers, and then put to death in a horrible way. The thighbones of both father and daughter he had made into handles for his cutlery, but the rest were pounded in a mortar together with their dried flesh, and this was distributed to the Samian mills where it was mixed in with the flour, so the population was made to eat it in their loaves of wheat.

After the death of Polycrates, Maeandrius became tyrant. At first he advertised himself as a liberator of the people and claimed to support an isonomous form of government. He had jars of wine opened in the streets and festoons of flowers placed over the gateways of the city; then built an altar to Zeus, Defender of Freedom, of whom he claimed himself to be the ambassador-priest; and at the Heraion he offered up all the sumptuous furniture of Polycrates' palace. However, he soon revealed his true character, refused to renounce the power he had gained and began to oppress the islanders, proscribing those citizens who had previously been most prominent at court, putting them to death in ignominious ways, quartering Telesarchus, impaling Polydor. He railed against Polycrates, soiled his memory with foul words, but neither he nor his words pleased the Samians who remembered their former ruler with fondness, because he had enriched them, and brought great things and glory to the island.

And so it was that when the Persians, with an army led by Otanes, arrived and attacked Samos, hardly a single one of the citizens, dispirited as they were and hating Maeandrius, would take up arms in its defence. . . . . . . And the Persians committed many outrages, looted and then fired the Heraion, slaughtered great numbers . . . . . . defeated Maeandrius, who escaped with much treasure [*to wander Greece with his impover-ished name*], replaced him on the throne with Syloson; and while that brother of the dead Polycrates feasted himself on endored heads of kids and salted hearts of ibex, while he communicated obscenities in languid tones to Pison, the temples fell into disrepair; the island became depopulated through his mismanagement; so the saying: "By the resolve of Syloson there is plenty of room."

Collapsing Claude

I.

The sun had already gone down; the lake was a dark, glassy sheet; the branches of the tree by which he stood dripped down into the water and a few pieces of driftwood and trash floated near the bank. Claude was still; he inhaled the breath of the flowers in the gardens behind him; watched the lights appear on the opposite shore; and things sank into night. He lit a cigarette and walked along the path, with the lake to his right. Twelve years of his life of twenty-nine he had spent endeavouring to put himself in certain situations; behind closed doors; in scented or filthy chambers; to experience the snorting adventures of a hog. He worked in a bank, and though not rich, certainly made a decent living.

He walked slowly, erect, stiffly. A nebulous patch, an obvious quantity of female, rose up from a park bench to one side. He stopped. The creature moved on in front of him. Claude proceeded, automatically to tail, now truly savouring that flavour of smoke in which he bathed his tongue. The serpent looked back (only the slightest exposure of facial flesh); then turned, some scarf over head; throat and mouth sheltered, shadow of trees and black blankness of night.

"Are you following me?"

"Yes."

A pause.

"Who are you?"

"A man named Claude."

Another pause.

"OK then. . . . A woman named Mirta."

"Do we need to know anything else?"

"Negative."

II.

And black turns piquant, red, that to the yolk-coloured light of a little bedside lamp. He made an involuntary movement back, in surprise; shuddered; his feet touched the floor.

Her breasts were distorted and flagging mounds of flesh; her skin-tone an overfed pink, like that of a sow. A hunched up beast reminiscent of an overgrown worm. With eyes that flashed hunger she scanned him, parted lips and laughed, revealing a wide pit of a mouth, spitting out coarse and guttural accents of amusement. And then she stopped; showed a tongue, like a piece of raw liver; rubbed one cheek against one of her shoulders.

"Do you like what you see?" she asked.

"You are disgusting," Claude replied; securing the

buckle of his belt.

III.

He had spent a good portion of the afternoon at the
Caffé Federale on the Piazza Riforma; a tall beer was
in front of him, a cigarette sat perched in the ashtray,
a slender wisp of smoke curling from it. Many beautiful
women walked by, lithe and fashionable blondes from
Germany, dark, full-breasted beauties from Italy, petite
and full-lipped lispers of France, and other packages of
flesh mortal.

But while his eyes saw, it was not of the beauties
he thought. His mind was continually pulled back to
the night previous, to the repulsive creature he had
encountered, who had dealt with him with such unparalleled skill.

Her little apartment, he could find his way there.

IV.

She fried sausages and served them with a cheap
Barbera. He watched her as she ate, stuffed the great
gash in her face, guzzled glasses of the purple liquid,
a few drops running from her lips like drops of blood.
And then she would grab his head between her hands,

a foul gust of air issuing from her mouth as she pressed it to his, sinking a thick and hot muscle down his own eager throat.

He was intoxicated by this horrible being; thrilled when she snatched and dragged him down to the unswept terra cotta floor, undulated her coils and let him roll on her belly, sink in the suet of her body; when he felt her dull teeth sink into the sinews of his neck.

She would murmur unheard of obscenities; and her avid words exhilarated Claude like a most pleasant electrical shock; his jaw would tremble, a thick and solitary tear, like hot wax, slip from one eye. Every evening spent with her aged him a year; small folds and lines appeared in the skin around his two eyes, which themselves had taken on the dull lustre of that black mineral called coal, decomposed bodies of prehistoric beasts and plants. His pectorals, which had been firm as iron, began to sag and take on the appearance of unattractive female breasts, and when he shaved, he now always seemed to miss a spot here or there so he was never without a little stray bit of beard sprouting from some angle of his chin.

"Move in with me; I will treat you well, buy you nice silk nighties!"

"You already supply me with enough see-through things."

V.

The offer of his own perverse heart on a salver constructed from his own suffused pelvic bones mere refreshment for her so fierce even often cruel with the flat of hand juggling of sharp and blunt words and curses and then letting him kiss her dewlaps as a thick semi-fluid substance oozed from her mouth. Distracted, restless during each day, he only wishing to spill himself into the night glory of letting her gnaw the lips from his face.

"No, don't come tonight. I have to go to Torino."

"Torino?"

What did she have to do in Torino?

He spent a nearly sleepless night perspiring solitary beneath his sheets. The next day, Sunday, he smoked countless cigarettes, toured the bars, sampled all the second-rate wines the city had to offer, seeing in the depth of each glass the burning labbra of Mirta; and he craved to feel the air of her flaring nostrils, hot as a desert wind, against his stomach and thighs.

Darkness; and standing beneath her window; but if she were there, in bed, there would probably be no light anyhow. He listened attentively, thinking he might hear some voice, or groan, from the story above him, through the glass or thick walls. There was a car engine in the distance; it faded; then silence. So he walked away, wandered along streets, the Corso Elvezia, the

Via Serafino Balestra, then found himself circling, back around to the Via Luigi Lavizzari, spying on her dwelling. He stood in an alcove, for several hours, and then finally, around four in the morning, made his way home, exhausted, thoroughly depressed.

The next day at work his face was pale and his eyes looked like raw sores. For lunch he had four rolls of shredded tobacco enclosed in thin paper and ignited and then, after work, drank several purple glasses followed by a grappino. He knew very well that Mirta was far from being honourable; she would not hesitate to lie, to him or anyone else; in his guts he felt that she had never gone out of town, but simply wanted to get rid of him; to have her pleasures in some other way. He slunk out onto the street; it was summer and still light; warm, and he wished for the sky to be black.

VI.

He stood again beneath her window and listened attentively to the ringing in his own ears; then crossed the street and took up his position in the alcove. He chewed on his bottom lip and then his tongue. The distant church bells sounded the hours, first three, then four, then five, then six.

"What's the use," he told himself morosely.

A hulkingly masculine figure came out the door and proceeded to walk down the street; the gait of an ape, a large and tailless monkey, with tight jeans and absurdly broad shoulders. Claude followed him. The man turned the corner and so did Claude. Then they were eye to eye. The man was there opening the door of a car.

"What do you want?"

"I'm Claude."

"So what? Do you think you deserve some kind of prize for it? Do I owe you money?"

"Mirta. . . . She's my girl."

The man laughed. "Get away from me or I'll break your nose," he said.

Claude hit him on the side of the head with his open hand. Then Claude was on the ground. The man sunk his huge fist into Claude's face; the latter's nose seemed to explode, turn into a mass of red jelly. And he felt the man's fist several more times, and the man's boot as well.

VII.

After making his way to the hospital, where he received numerous stitches, he returned home, lay on the couch and cried. The woman-hunter in him, the man who sought out the beds of the females of the species for mere sport, seemed to be dying a tragic death; the body of Claude was now animated by a variety of weak and needy soul, a soul that cried out for Mirta's stroke and affection, squealed to be treated to her coarse favours, ridden by her lard and grotesque self; and, exhausted from sleepless nights and unnatural emotional tension, he slept, dreamt of her as a great hippopotamus, her huge butt-like breasts spangled with a thousand greasy nipples and, crawling out from betwixt her gargantuan thighs, a multitude of beasts; a writhing viper of three heads; a slippery shark snapping at the air with blood-drenched fangs; a creature half scorpion and half man; a four-winged demon of storms who breathed hurricanes and pissed tidal waves; a dragon with the front feet of a cat and, for hind feet, the claws of a bird and a body shining with lubriciously wet scales; and others of complex and difficult to describe anatomy, some with huge proboscises, others with giant, flailing ears.

VIII.

Knowing that the man was there, holding tight to her wads of flesh, made him want her all the more; desire to sniff even the stench of their love making.

"Oh, you are back," she said, opening the door. She was wearing a transparent night-gown made out of some kind of synthetic material. It was not one of the garments he had bought her, but something cheaper, utterly whorish. "Your face does not look good. Not such a pretty boy anymore are you?"

"Is he here?"

"Egon? No, he is back in Berlin now."

"But . . ."

"Shut up and come in. I know you have been craving me."

He entered and kissed her neck.

"I found a new place to live, a villa, and I want you and Egon to both be my roommates."

"You want us all to move in together?"

"I have to get out of here dammit!" she cried peevishly. "The neighbours . . . they won't stop complaining about the noise we make. . . . *Merde*! Do you think I should have to put up with that?"

"But all of us together," Claude said sullenly.

"Well, if you don't want to join us!"

"This new place, how much is the rent?"

"Four-thousand francs a month. Your share is twenty-five hundred."

"But four-thousand divided by . . ." The words died on his lips.

Mirta gave him an ominous look. "I don't need to hear any complaints from you, boy. If you don't like the arrangements you can just piss off." And then she softened, her mood changed, she smirked. "Of course I only wanted to do it for you. . . . You had been complaining because I did not move in with you. . . . And then in the evening I might cook some nice meals for the three of us. . . . Raclette. . . . Lovely roast rabbit. . . . Lean flesh of ass."

IX.

The place was giant, old and dirty, though grand in an infernal sort of way. Claude went from threshold to threshold, room to room, his voice echoing through the corridors and down the vast staircase. He cleaned, expended money on furniture and painted the walls himself, while Egon sat back, drank beer and grunted out instructions in German. He talked about football matches and told of how he had once killed a man in Hamburg by hitting him over the head with a cinder-block. Then Mirta would come in, exuding an odour of rancid grease, wearing tight leather trousers that emphasised her disgusting bulk; she would slide her tongue down Egon's throat and then approach Claude, slap his flanks, pull his head down to her bosom while she loaded him with gross epithets.

She was a demon who could crush men with her enormous bulk, destroy them with her sexual favours, a weapon was her very loins. Even when she was not physically there, he still felt some mass of congealed air around him; and prayed, on knees, with forehead glued to the ground, that he might hear her climactic bellow.

When he came home from work he was made to wear a cowbell about his neck and crawl around the house naked; the sound always alerted Mirta when he was near. Once, only once, he had the audacity to stuff the bell with hygienic tissue, but he was discovered and

Egon beat him with a curtain rod. The hot meals he had been promised, the raclette, the roast rabbit, never appeared; instead, like a dog he was fed food from a can. She dressed him up like a clown, made him perform tricks like a trained seal. His dignity was flayed; at work he stooped like a hunchback and his colleagues avoided him; the boss had already reprimanded him twice for his slovenly appearance and distracted air; he was sure to be terminated before long.

And then summer ended and it was fall.

Rains came, day after day, and washed away the sides of hills, whole houses, parts of small villages. The lake ran over and threw its garbage and driftwood up over the embankments. Claude, during his lunch break, walked along the shore, through the park where he had first met her and then along the Viale Carlo Cattaneo. At the Viale Cassarate he stood on the bridge and stared down into the water. It was chocolate-brown and violent. It threw up liquid arms and dripping hands that seemed to grab, to want to pull him down, along, under. A whole tree drifted by. And he leaned over, tempted, and sacrificed several tears to the raging demon, which were mixed, broken into a trillion fragments, and thrown into the lake beyond.

He walked into the church, Santa Maria degli Angeli, sat down and wept. His bleary eyes looked up at the fresco there, that done by Bernardino Luini, of Christ Jesus crucified, but the work, the bright colours, the images of thieves, the sponge full of vinegar upraised on a reed, only made him feel more desperate.

X.

Egon, in the form of a great ox, suckled at her breast; he wore a crown plumed with ostrich feathers and on his back the skin of a panther. Claude saw her coupling with centaurs, fat-haunched satyrs, a minotaur; wallowing in pools of pus, her indecent body riveted by the lusts of countless beasts and devils. He woke up and walked to her room. Egon was there, wearing nothing but a pair of shorts, his back, chest and legs were covered with thick black hair, like that of a wild animal. She lay twisted on the floor, the victim, of herself, of some brutal and perverted episode she had shared with the man. He turned, stared at Claude with dull, bloodshot eyes and Claude, frightened, slammed the door shut and then ran out onto the street screaming for the police like a woman.

XI.

Later, after Egon had been extradited back to Germany and sent to prison, Claude would take the train, visit him, bring cartons of cigarettes, offerings of wool socks, and beg to hear about her.

"She was a hellhole," Egon would say, staring

through the Plexiglas barrier with stupid eyes. "A damn hellhole . . . always got my chicken roasted."

And then Claude, stuttering out his words, asked for specifics; he wanted that imprisoned golem to speak of every oily detail, of Mirta and her games.

XII.

Wearing a blue wool vest and pants that terminated at the ankles, pants brown with dirt on the knees and rump, he would walk along the cobbled streets. The dark pits of his eyes, the drooping of his lower lip, were all signs, of the complete collapse of the inner man. And then at home, in the little apartment he had moved into, he spent his time slapping his own face, fantasising about her, flinging the last of his manhood into the latrine.

He was abject, finished, because he would never find a woman half so disgusting as Mirta, and even his imagination was insufficient to supply the filth.

The Dancing Billionaire

Art thou poor, yet hast thou golden slumbers?
O sweet content!
Art thou rich, yet is thy mind perplex'd?
O punishment!

—Thomas Dekker

I.

"I am afraid that he is an ineffectual boy."

"Is a boy meant to be effectual? What exactly is it you expect him to effect?"

"I have always hoped that he would become more . . . strident."

"You have strange ambitions and, pardon my saying, unrealistic expectations. Every human being has its own temperament,—an artistic nature should not be manhandled."

"I have the ambitions of a father. A man does not like to see his son peter out so early in life."

"I did not notice that he had ever petered on. To me he simply seems like a rather frail boy. He may not have the over——Well, the same bearing as his father, but he is a nice enough child. Have some sympathy for him Ralph. A man should love his offspring."

The man and woman walked over the grounds, and though one man, one woman, they were the same of nose, of gesture, the family's eyes, brownish beads floating on oval faces, jaws ever so slightly salient. . . . They rise on their toes, their gait uplifting in aspiration, uncapped pride. . . . Sun, moon; organs sexual, jointly different, german; beads quivering down the atavistic rosary, dropped from ovaries consanguineous, spermazoa mutual, produced in similar sessions of grave copulation.

II.

The child stood alone on the lawn beside the great house. You know that the sky was blue, that there were a few white clouds. You know that the weather was warm, and all around the smell of fresh cut grass.

He heard the laughter, from an open window, and knew that they, the adults, were within,—drinking things that he could not drink, bitter sweet, the cause of that mild, quaint delirium.

He walked to the tennis court and watched the groundskeeper pull minute weeds from the cracks. The man looked up and smiled at him, a little sadly, and he, condescendingly, smiled back.

With arms folded the child kicked his toe against the court—a piquant spasm of dissatisfaction—and studied the other opposite him: The man on hands and knees, his years doing little to distinguish him from the worm of the earth, the groping creature of the soil. A bird sang from a nearby tree. The young, upright human both enjoyed and respected that beauty of nature, though he might despise the callousness of man.

The groundskeeper, whose name was Oliver, took up the bucket of weeds he had pulled and walked to the flower garden. The child, whose name was Allen, followed him, without speaking. He watched in silent disdain and interest as Oliver weeded around the French marigolds, of which there was a full bed. He could smell the pregnant, female earth, but was not tempted to touch it, just as he liked the brown back of the man's neck, wrinkled and rough, without desire for more intimate knowledge of its texture.

A butterfly fluttered by Allen, landing amid nearby carnations. He snuck up to it and grabbed it in his pale and delicate hands, crushing it, painting them with the powder of its wings.

"A painted lady," he lisped, letting the corpse drop to the ground.

*

His father, thick-figured, moustached, hair tending to mouse colour, a small glass of hard drink in hand; his father laughed, the sound swelling from deep in his torso, organic; teeth showing, a cigar rolling between fingers, smoke magnetizing toward the ceiling. . . . Allen saw the eyes meet him, momentarily, traitors of the man's apprehension. . . . Yes, he, Ralph, was made nervous by that thin, China-white manikin standing there, that pompous sprout of unwanted fibre, that child against nature, even at such a young age haloed by an aura of self-satisfaction. God knows he must have questioned his wife's fidelity, or put all the blame on her sickly, inbred line. But maybe that woman's weakness, her frailty of carriage, her demi-royal descent, had been the real, original attraction. Was not love that melting confusion, recklessness, of contorted limbs, slavering of eyes, words said and compression of hopes to pain?

There were those suited giants, billowy women, enjoyment, or what adults call enjoyment, seek for. And in the library, where he wandered to with surly steps, a piece of marzipan in hand, dissolving in his mouth, creamed along his gums; in the library he saw her sitting. A girl about his own age, a large picture book on her lap.

"Hello," he said.

The scrutiny on his part was obvious, lids half closed, mouth slowly churning.

"There is more in the kitchen," he remarked.

"More?"

"There is more marzipan in the kitchen, if that's what you want. I won't get it for you, but it is sitting there,—a whole bowl of it."

"I don't like marzipan, and I'm not to eat sweets except at dessert," her girl's voice, crisp with English accent, upper class cadence.

And then there was his aunt, echoing from without, calling his name.

"Allen!" she cried, as she came blowing through the

door. "There you are Allen. . . . There you are children," her eyes wide with eccentricity.

III.

You were very near being a naughty boy—a boy one might have called atrocious, except that you had such pretty skin, such winning ways when it pleased you to charm.

Remember, it was I who took you clothes shopping, to indulge my broken feminine streak, if you wish to call it so. . . . But I did enjoy expending my taste. — Yes, I was born with a few lumps of that—on suiting you elegantly, protecting your genteel instincts. . . . Of course I realise that you got them from her. There is not a marked degree of refinement on my side of the family. Still, I have always recognized and respected beauty when it condescended to enter my sphere. And, believe me, I mean to imply no negative undertones.

—But you did look so cute, in your little garments, selected by me, my chapped hands; a little gentleman. And then we styled your hair. . . . You were my doll, the baby doll of a big, greying girl,—you were much more to me.

IV.

Allen Hutton appears in a violet jacket, an avocado tie, terminating a full three inches above his waistline, and a simple fine-weave cotton shirt of the lightest shade of blue. His pants, tan, immaculately pressed, form two slashes above black booties.

Guests mingle, thin-stemmed glasses growing from hands like effervescent fungi. Women gossip over diminutive plates of mulberry salad, Vicksburg cheese balls, and aspic-glazed shrimp. Here a fashion is made of laziness and many smile, for they can fathom, in their spoon-like existences, no reason to frown: a woman with the head of a sheep plugged on the neck of a turtle talks in low tones to a gentleman resembling, to a startling degree, a well groomed summer sausage. An ex-senator staggers unsteadily by, the flesh of his face flopping behind a protruding jowl. A hired pianist, placed discretely off to one side, plays Chopin, a sub-servient smile freezing his blanched and meager lips.

Allen, standing hipshot before the bar, was just taking the first sip of his Alexander and noting the strangeness of the group of guests his father and aunt had assembled when she herself, the aunt, appeared, pulling him off to one side.

"I would like to introduce you to someone," she said. "Or I should say re-introduce. I believe that you met as children. . . . Allen Hutton, Lady Helen Ashe."

"A lady . . . well," he said, taking her fingertips and signaling mock deference with a downward inclination of his head.

"Helen is the Earl of Saxelby's daughter," Aunt Margaret remarked.

"Yes, I remember," Allen commented suavely. "And how is the Right Honourable Earl? I seem to recall visiting some old castle of his, on a greenish sort of hillside, a lot of long shrubbery, a bit depressing. But maybe I am being too forward. I remember you, but you might not remember me. This violet jacket throws people."

"To be frank, the violet jacket was the only thing I did think I recognized."

Large-kneed Aunt Margaret smiled nervously as she looked at the two, both so attractive, both so much more feminine than she.

*

Later, as the guests began to filter out, Mr. Hutton took Allen apart to the study. Lighting a cigarette and leaning his healthy rump against a desk he proceeded:

"Allen, I am going to broach a subject which I know is distasteful to you, but you are going to have to face sometime, and I believe now is as good as any."

"Father, really," the young man replied, throwing his body into the soft, cool mass of a leather armchair.

"Occupation Allen. You have to choose some kind of occupation. At school you took in a pretty good variety of directionless classes: film appreciation, Greek drama, dancing for God's sake! . . . Don't you realise that your family is sitting on a fortune; a fortune which it takes outrageous energy and prudence to manage, to maintain, grow. . . . A great deal of responsibility . . ."

Allen looked on with raised eyebrows and an amused expression.

"You don't expect me to work, do you?" he asked.

"I not only expect you to work, but to make something of yourself. It is obvious that business does not appeal to you at present. Fine. You're young. Time will undoubtedly show you its value. But for now, choose some occupation, some honourable occupation, and follow it. . . . So . . . What do you want to do? Tell me."

"Shop."

"Excuse me?"

"Shop . . . I really do like clothes you know. I could spend a few years inspecting the various boutiques and—"

"Enough," his father, Ralph Hutton, cried out. "Being a clothes horse is not an occupation. It is a moral failing. Now *what* are you going to do with yourself?"

The younger man rolled his eyes back in his head, and stroked his moustache. The role of son bored him. The things he liked were not tasks but fantasies. There was pleasure, the absurd and the sensual; there was what could be paid for and what he did not care to touch; and other things he was willing to sample.

V.

Bipeds moved along the streets of the city, many bearing themselves with the ease of the financially secure; the smile of laziness adhered to faces; women's puffed lips strangely decorous: we see opulence and laugh, hear the languages of the world warbled. And then the click of Italianate shoes, red heels gliding over the deeper shade of brick. Eccentric he was, walking as if those around him did not exist, were invisible, certainly not worth notice. But her, strangely his wife, honeymoon fresh, if not dripping sweet, bizarre.

Before the glass panes of a jewellery establishment, whose reputation was not in the least exaggerated, Allen stopped, the woman following suit.

"What a gorgeous display," he said.

The Etruscan fibula shaped like a twisted pelican; the bracelet a golden serpent eating its own tail, eyes of sphene, body marked with red enamel; earrings, thin, sunny disks showing the river god Achelous; a necklace, each bead a golden, pregnant woman, each womb a semiprecious stone; and that tiara, simple, like a cluster of aspen leaves in fall.

"I want you to have them," Allen said, an odd sparkle in his eyes. "The entire collection. . . . My wedding present. . . . To you."

"I don't think this is the kind of jewellery one actually *wears*," she commented.

"Of course it is. You'll wear it," he said, going through the door.

*

"Undress," he said.

She blushed, guardedly satisfied, breasts stiffened, risen. The dress dropped from her shoulders, girdle unfastened, drawers, like a crumpled petal of orchid, lay at her feet. She stood, legs pressed together, a white, bare stroke of apparent virginity, a conflux of drooling stars.

I am molten love, she knew. *I am a sea anemone, a fluctuating bubble of blood. I am in need, of taking, entwining, wrapping my boneless limbs around, burping gorgeous obscenities—I am snow-coated coal—I am a moonlit well—I am naked, a woman, beauty of woman, in long of love. I am me. I am me.*

"Put the jewels on now," he said.

"Jewels?"

"The diamonds, the necklace, that lovely bracelet. And, oh yes—the tiara, the tiara."

His voice hoarse.

"You *are* a funny one," she said.

She felt them cold against her skin, grinning around her neck, licking her wrists, lashed to her head. She felt something spook around her, enter into her, as yet undefined, inscrutable . . .

She walked toward him, feeling the carpet beneath her feet.

"No," he said. "Just stay there. Let me look at you."

"I am cold."

"Stay there! The jewellery is so wonderful. It really is."

Pleasure unsought, untasted. Breasts of bread, thighs, joining in a bottomless pit that yet bears reflection; a bubbling slug. Perversion, the skinless dog of art, crawls, flesh bare, an exposed and living wound, salivating magenta, pools of slick filth.

And, to awake in humiliation,—that fear of the living being—her hair heavy as that final departure into night, and tears, the swelling of pus of nightmares.

VI.

Denny held the mushroom stuffed with duck sausage between two fingers.

"You've come into it," he said. "Of course it *is* in bad taste to word it that way. But amongst friends. And, you know, money can be a real consolation at a time like this."

He bit into the mushroom cap and chewed, his eyes, those of a voluptuary, half closed. There was no denying that Pellington could cook. Allen was tolerable company, but Denny's primary interest was in the food.

"I feel rather despondent," said Allen as he sipped his mint julep. It was difficult to add appropriate gravity to the action. "I would cry if I knew it would help."

"Yes," said Denny, that young gentleman with short maize-coloured hair, an extremely delicate tan, a feathery voice and much appreciation for his own beauty, "I would shed tears with you if I knew it would help. But it won't. It won't help at all. So we must not spoil our lunch on some fruitless, rather straining endeavor. A quick cry would not add the smallest bit of enjoyment to this mushroom stuffed with duck sausage. . . . Life is for the living. We should always remember that."

After inhaling the last morsel of mushroom he sliced an asparagus spear into three parts, wondering if he should not take a bite of crab cake before proceeding.

"Yes," clipping off a chunk of the crab cake with his fork after surmising that the asparagus would undoubtedly wait for him. "Yes, my heart goes out to you Allen, but we must find a way to distract our minds from morbid thoughts, depression. Good dining and sophisticated company are a starting point."

VII.

Your mother, what she would think, I cannot guess. I did not love her, I will admit that, but do not press me for more. . . . Your father cared for her, and I saw that she was elegant, refined—Oh, she had much of what I lacked.

But do not think that any of . . . of that emotional disarray. —Do not think that it has prejudiced me against you. No, I have always been your strongest advocate, and will defend you, even if it were to mean draining my veins dry of their sap. —Yes, you are a handsome, so handsome young man.

   —Allen, I will be there for you, when you have discarded fresher blooms.

VIII.

He had always liked theatre, movies, dancing, entertainment of all description as long it tended toward the benign, the sensual. Astair was a well-tailored god; *Swing time, Top Hat,* ecstatic suavity. Allen Hutton's face would burn with the flush of blood, then grow suddenly pale, the tapping, the orchestra crying into the secret places of his being—Fred Astair dancing off chairs, tables, desks, steps, dogs, walls, ceilings; the perfectly cut suit never gathering up, the sunshine smile never betraying the whisper of death.

   In the subdued light of the movie room Allen lay on his side, one elbow embedded in a soft pillow, a hand supporting his weary head. The stem of a hookah extended from his sentient lips. . . . The screen before him, of generous proportion—women blooming into flowers, the petals of their lower limbs, and those stamen arms; *Golddiggers of 1938*; one-thousand legs lashing as whips, the sex subdued into patterns of cosmic grandeur. . . . Sets of dreams, opulence of love beyond his grasp. . . . Busby Berkeley, took away his body, those instants, tender as the skin of boiled milk.

And in his study he would sometimes read the first few lines of Helen's letters in disgust. But more often than not he simply threw them away unopened. And then, to Allen's relief, they stopped. . . . Subsequently only vague reports, of the woman's frantic, sluttish romances with Portuguese gigolos and decaying aristocratic rakes.

IX.

"Do you want me to be saucy, or submissive?"

"Surprise me," Allen said, with a gesture worthy of a Caesar, yellowish smoke spiraling from the Turkish oval balanced between his fingertips.

The creature was at his feet, nestled up and caressing his calves. Allen bent, letting his hand scrub through the short black hair.

"Li Chi, you little beast, demean yourself."

The slobber ran from the young man's mouth as he raised that pants' leg, licking shin and kneecap. Allen laughed weakly at the contortions below him. The face lifted, two teardrops arrested, then rolling from the eyes.

"Why do you weep my child?" voice saccharine, darkly soothing.

The mouth opened, explained: . . . His wife, children, family . . . in China . . . so poor. . . . He was an astrologer . . . not a love toy. . . . The honour of his family. . . . He sent them money . . . but . . .

"You're not a love toy?" cried Allen. "Finding that there was no work in the first world for an astrologer, you advertised, I responded. Tears of remorse were not part of the bargain. . . . Pout you dog!"

His walking stick was at hand. He struck viciously, excited by the squeals induced. The corrupt fist tensed white. Expensive paste of raw man.

When he, Allen, left the house, his face was decorated with a plastic smile. Dressed to the perfection of his taste, he strode to the flower garden. The carnations were in full bloom, their scent heavy through the air. Oliver was there, crawling amidst the stalks.

Allen, without speaking a word to the old gardener, plucked a blossom and stuck it in the button hole of his jacket. Whistling, he made his way to the garage, the shadow of his body crossing over the other man, a black mass; like some slow-moving buzzard that passed overhead.

X.

Like a rattlesnake are the cabasas, the hands holding them moving rhythmically through the cuffs of a garish gold shirt. There are four of these sentinels, men dressed like the sun, bodies jerking, swaying, aggregating, dispensing music Latin,—sticks and palms frolic on drums, fingers flit over keys, slam, press until knuckles bend. The voices join up, swelling Spanish, an inundation of ebon joy. Coloured lights flash pathetically over bobbing heads; smiles on most; a few serious men, lips gravitated to decorous frowns. One young man, in jeans skintight and a blousy shirt, moves his arms like a windmill, one leg bent, taught, angular. An older woman flings herself in tribal indecorum before a young partner of indeterminate sex. Limbs madly wag, pulsate and reach like a cage full of millipedes.

Li Chi sat at a corner table, slowly drinking a Corona. His eyes rested blankly on the dance floor, on Allen salsa dancing with a young woman in a tight red tank top. She thrust her small, pigeon-like breasts toward him, flapped her arms like chicken wings. Her eyebrows, extremely black, acted as bees floating above the ochre calyxes of her irises. Enchanted, Allen Hutton displayed his best footwork, took her by one hand, smiled as her arm passed over his head; her body quickly circumnavigated his.

He was slumming. Over the course of a few months he had passed through many of the low bars and dance-halls, discothèques, drunk. movement. energy. design. The folk dances of the peasants, vulgar cha-cha, salsa at Enrico's, the waltz, a resurgence of the fashion of ballroom dancing. . . . The earliest form of artistic and personal expression; the prehistorics thus worshipped gods, petitioned for success on the battlefield, the hunting ground; to celebrate birth, heal the sick, mourn for the dead. . . . Allen practised the various mudras of the art, thought himself rather brave to frequent spheres where most were of darker coloured skin than he, the rich and delicate white man. . . . A cloud, infectious heat, the people, heady vapour of nescience.

Plato recommended, urged, all Greek citizens to take up the art.

XI.

A)
Nephew, when you came, into my room of a sudden. . . . I blush at the recollection. —Let me admit it, my shame is streaked with pleasure.

What did you think though, of your aunt revealed, of her desire unsheathed.

Child, child.

B)
Because she, not unlike some strange and enormous unfertilized insect, virgin martyr, first in awe of her older brother, Ralph Hutton (intrigued by, almost attracted to his wife) and then (when that one was no more) a profoundly tender and passionate affection developed within her for pale young Allen (he saw her without the usual covering, the usual pastels, flower-patterned dress; atrocious accident). . . . The woman's feelings existing in a strange no-man's-land, unclaimed, impossible to define, intelligent thought certainly mixed with dark unsexed lusts and animal hungers,

that haze of secret desires which never was exposed to the world, but which stewed constantly within her, made her bosom swell.

XII

The invitations to Allen's debut caused more than a few eyebrows to rise in the best society. Yet, an evening's amusement was a given; for amusing it *would* be.

So as gentlemen knotted their ties before mirrors and women felt the sheerness of the stockings ascend their legs, conjecture was given as to the nature of the entertainment. The little square of gilt-edged, maroon invitation received through the mail described it simply as "A Musical and Theatrical Extravaganza."

*

Against a background of painted profiles, sandy stone and a distant oasis, he appears, the Queen of the Nile. A tight dress of hand-dyed cotton sets off his slim yet not unmanly figure, from beneath which emerge two feet adorned in simple sandals; a reddish-gold headdress serves as crown; precious jewellery adorns his waist, wrists, neck and ears; the nails of his fingers and toes are painted the colour of claret, while, beneath his thick moustache, abide lips painted a dark shade of pink; eyes outlined in circles of swamp-green, eyebrows coloured leaden-grey.

Music strikes up, serpentine, flute and violin, rattle

and tabla.

Rather a ditch in Egypt be gentle grave unto me! Rather on Nilus' mud lay me stark nak'd, and let the water-flies blow me into abhorring! Rather make my country's high pyramids my gibbet, and hang me up in chains!

Next tableau:

The curtains glide open.

He appears, cane in hand, in black coat and tails, bow tie, top hat, tipped negligently to one side, and spats.

The orchestra bursts forth, coolly, his mouth drops open, utters words of song, strangely pathetic, ridiculously melancholy.

guests twist
that embarrassed sweat
glistening brows of red madness

Stepping out with my baby . . .

The cane toyed with, an extension of the procreative obsession, violins
waves of colourful insects.

smooth sailing 'cause I'm trimming my sails . . .

Third:

From the sidelines a dulcet but delusively virile voice:

Down in the West Texas town of El Paso . . .

He immerges, from the cactus-flecked desert, grimly romantic, in a tight and black silk dress flaring out at the base, over the clicking heels . . .

I fell in love with a Mexican girl.

Gliding across the stage, ultra-serious, eyes half closed in fervour . . .

Nighttime would found me at Rosie's cantina . . .

The dance is performed, strongly reminiscent of the death throws of a butterfly, a burnt insect.

. . . nice señorita . . .

The bellows huffing in the fear, well guarded panic,
taps, bullets of decadence
the porcelain shatters
his eyes left lidless
independent and moist beings.

XIII.

He sat, looking at the room around him, the high ceilings, oblong blocks of light thrust through the windows, shaded darker where intercepted by the bangs of curtain. The pedestal on which sat the bronze hands did nothing for him; he had paid one hundred thousand dollars; Bruce Nauman's name was a name, but his hands, at that moment, were empty of life, let alone lust for it.

He looked at his own, bony, white, ten tentacles of sensitive desperation; a wedding ring still banded to one, from that farce; lunacy.

Rising, his legs circumambulated the chamber, past the coffee table, select magazines spread in fan-shaped perfection, the stone statue of Uma, the flamboyant Gilbert & George. . . . He caressed the leaves of a few tropical plants, and looked fondly at the Venus' fly trap, the fanged chartreuse. . . . In front of the high windows he found himself, overlooking the estate, the gardens.

He could see Oliver out there, under a straw hat, back bent, hands moving in slow, regular motions. The ageing man had spent those years there, amongst the plants, a friend of the trees, collecting soil beneath his fingernails, his face webbed with wrinkles from the sun.

There are these creatures, believed Allen, who take up tasks, work at contemptible, obscure trades, squeezed like rags, swept aside like dirt. Before the dawn breaks they crawl out of their kennels, wear their heels thin against abrasive streets—some off to waitress in diners to the smell of burnt suet—delivery boys eking out a pittance hauling ill burgers and sandwiches up through high rises, skyscrapers—scroungers, cripples, begging for quarters . . . men who pick up trash for a living . . . butchers whacking at thick red meat. . . . There are those who lay bricks, paint houses, mix cement, clothes worn and splattered, arms thick with plebian strength. Others, women, selling wares behind counters, answering telephones, putting on bright, silly smiles, for what they call a wage, for a few worthless rectangles of paper. . . . Yes, people sew and set bones, try cases in miserable court, douse out fires, cuff criminals, tinker on ridiculous machinery, scrambling like insects, poisoned like roaches. . . . And then there are groundskeepers, gardeners. . . . And those who keep them and watch them sweat.

Later he saw his aunt. They dined together. He talked, tried to give voice to his emptiness, said that he felt like a hollow pot.

Aunt Margaret's nostrils quivered. Her eyes were moist, languorous. "Yes," she murmured, placing her hand atop Allen's, "my life also seems empty."

Allen, self-involved, self-centred, did not seem to notice the relative's half muffled, fully desperate emotion.

"There is always travel," he said.

"Yes . . . we could . . . you might . . . travel."

"India." Thinking of the land of self-revelation; for

one pampered since birth on every material object conducive to sumptuous living the raw struggles of the world held a sudden attraction, as some cheeses, offensive of smell and crawling with maggots, are the most savoury; with vague images of renunciation coated in pink sugar and perfumed with sandalwood, served with smooth blue-skinned youths stuffed with juicy slices of bright orange mango.

". . . to discover myself . . . travel alone . . . I believe that is requisite for a spiritual sort of quest."

"Yes," said Aunt Margaret, "I believe it is," and she felt her lips grow cold, could hardly keep from uttering inarticulate sounds of suffering, keep from letting drops of saline, watery fluid flow from her eyes, throwing herself wildly at his feet even if it meant being butchered by his scorn.

XIV.

"Would you like something to drink with your meal?" asked the first-class stewardess, displaying the seemingly prefabricated smile of her trade.

The meal consisted of a slight mound of diced vegetables of questionable origin, tasting as if seasoned with ground copper, cooked by some nefarious process. . . . A chunk of flesh abiding beneath a semenish sauce,— poultry produced in a test tube, devoid alike of skin, bone, texture and flavour. . . . A salad of sickly forage, hardly fit for the snout of a pig. . . . Dessert, a brownie, chemically sweet.

The man sitting next to Allen—a hairless cranium loosely placed on a great ball of fat—had set to the mastication process with undisguised vigour, apparently well satisfied with the fare. . . . Allen merely dipped his fork into the substance; the odour made him undeniably queasy. He regretted having not arranged for a private flight.

"A cloudberry liquor," he told the young woman, his pale temples dewed with perspiration.

When the head of blonde hair shook, negating his request, and strawberry-coloured lips opened, expressing the actual state of the alcohol selection, Allen knew that he was amidst savages, on a downward course through trials and sufferings.

Sufficing himself, morosely, with a whisky sour, he curled up toward the window, withdrawing his organ of smell away from the bovine aroma that surrounded his neighbour. Down below he could see what he believed to be Pakistan, or Iran, an immense stretch of desert, pock-marked like the surface of the moon,— dried up canals scoring it, lonely hills casting blotches of shadow,—yellows, reds and browns, —tranquil, verdureless landscape.

He swallowed at the mixture in his hand, trying hard, desperately, to repress all thought. . . . The reason he was flying. Uncertainty, crawling through him like a caterpillar. Images entering, then fleeing his mind . . . of debauch, power, shame.

XV.

When he returned, his cheeks were hollow, his moustache an enormous black and misshapen patch, like Indian ink spilt on fresh-fallen snow. The wilderness of his eyes revealed nothing,—they were inscrutable, at times shining like tin in the sun, then becoming suddenly dull, lifeless as those of a frozen fish.

A solid gold Genesh now hung from his neck, its four arms swimming beneath his throat, its trunk and the viper curling around its body seeming to curve with undulations of mystical life. When Li Chi innocently asked about it, Allen's face grew ashen, his lips tightened, he drew further into himself, scurrying off, shutting his unsteady body within the walls of the library, out of which were heard groans and the sound of weeping.

Later, he emerged like a beast, threw a half dozen of his best suits in the fireplace and ignited them. With quick, whip-like words he dismissed all but the most necessary staff. He wrote a check for a large sum, flung it at Li Chi, and, with a voice shrill as a bird's cry, sent him packing.

Savagely he strode from room to room, hands clasped behind back, his hair flying with impetuous motion. The mansion seemed too small for his flurry, for the breadth of his shame. How much he would have liked to have spit out his suffering like the pit of an olive. Thoughts of severe acts of penance rode through his heated mind. He could picture himself stripped naked, rolling across North America, over the busy highways of the East Coast, through the Midwest, past thousands of miles of corn, the skin rubbed clean off his flesh, him spiraling over the Rocky Mountains, into California, his body one open sore,—sand, pebbles, bits of broken glass embedded in his carcass. . . . Or else he could sleep on a bed of nails, prostrate on razor blades, brush his teeth with a butcher's knife, bath in burning coals. . . . In India, from his hotel window, he had seen men, there on the public streets, saw off their limbs, howl out mantras, prayers, while the blue bottle flies thickened around their bleeding stumps, a few devalued coins occasionally clinking before them, from the hands of a passerby. . . . Others, on pilgrimages, hooks buried in their sides, carts attached to the hooks, the weight of the load stressing the meat of the body, creating open holes, pliable and repugnant. . . . Yes, he could see himself running through the streets, flogging himself with tassels of wet leather, a crown of thorns on his head, thick, sappy blood drooling down his face. . . . Because, after all, it seemed to him as if those emaciated ascetics he had witnessed were, if not happy, certainly content,—something he had never been. And then his ego had been attacked; he had unsystematically read, perused in confused incomprehension, countless ashramic and indological publications, crypto-Buddhistic, overtly Jainist—poor, outdated translations from the

Prakrit, the Pali, the Sanskrit, which spoke of libera-
tors of living beings, the practice of diverse penances
devoid of a desire for acquisition in paudgalic terms,
the ever-peaceful soundless and of infinite sounds, the
sameness, the illusory nature of waking and dream
states;—so a vague, not quite solidified question now
haunted his mind: If the objects cognized in both those
conditions are illusory, who is it who cognizes them
and who is it who imagines them?

XVI.

A)

*I am willing, even more than willing, to take the full
responsibility for all your little quirks. For me they are
so many lovely things; they are things that I admire
and believe the world should relish. . . . You are you,
never be another; rest awhile, and then visit me, in my
humble temple.*

*Others say that you could never love, but they have
not nurtured you, my sprout, my tree. Are you my all?*

*Just think on me once in a while, and try not to
forget the woman who sheltered and taught. There are
still deep chasms for me to bridge for you. Walk my
body underfoot; there is no need to be gentle.*

B)

. . . as she, buried her head in his shirts, sniffed at his

discarded socks, slept with a lock of his hair beneath her pillow. . . . It was an obsession, single-minded, that strangled the life from any real, material affection she might have ventured on; and even in the future, when her withered breasts would hang limply from her chest and her back would be bent, that pathetic fantasy would continue, as the most bitter and true pleasure of her life.

XVII.

Denny waited in the library of the great house, one leg draped over the next, a French cigarette hanging from his lax fingers. He had not been invited to lunch, or dinner, or an evening party. He had not been invited at all and had no expectations of receiving exotic nourishment from Pellington's kitchen. He was there solely for Allen—for his supposed benefit.

For Denny to be concerned with anyone but Denny, the situation must have been grave.

"Make yourself at home," said Allen as he walked in, his feet dragging lazily in slippers, body entrenched in a silk paisley bathrobe. "I wasn't expecting you. . . . Might have called before coming."

"No. I might not have. You might not have let me come."

"Well, you came, were let in the front door,—so that's about it. But I may as well tell you,—it's Pellington's day off."

"It decimates me to hear that I will not be fed a reasonable lunch, but the real reason that I'm here is to talk about you, my friend."

"Well, it seems to me you've picked the wrong person to talk to then. The best policy, generally speaking, is to talk about someone behind their back, not straight at them."

Denny took a long drag of his French cigarette, and, exhaling, said, "But you see, you are not a general case, you're peculiar. . . . Don't look so faux-shocked. Rumours have been spreading themselves through the social circuit that you're going a bit . . . well, whack-o to put it bluntly. . . . People are saying that you're turning into a sort of Howard Hughes. . . . And by the way, you needn't fib to me about Pellington. I know very well that you let him go. He came to my door with the whole story. . . . Told me about all kinds of monstrous things you wanted him to serve you. . . . Plain rice and unseasoned vegetables. . . . Really! . . . Naturally I hired him on the spot. Of course, when you come around you can have him back. Only a truly mad man would let a fellow like Pellington go. . . . In other words, if it was not for this gross proof I might not have believed the rumours."

The silence lasted several minutes. Denny extinguished the butt of his French cigarette and lit another. Allen circled the room slowly in his slippers, hands tucked in the pockets of his night robe.

"Denny," he said, stopping abruptly and looking fervently at the other man. "Denny, have you ever considered that there might be something more important in life than choosing whether to wear the apricot tie with the beige sports jacket or the mauve?"

"Well," Denny replied, "I have always considered the fruit shades to be out of the question in neckwear. As for mauve, I do believe I owned a tie of that colour some time ago—I think it got misplaced. . . . Why, have you seen it?"

"The point was not about the ties exactly. You see, I'm fed up . . . with life. . . . Ambitions come to nothing. My money will not buy me happiness you know."

"A startling revelation. I hope you haven't been sticking your nose in Thomas Merton again. Trust me, you would make a ludicrous desert father. . . . Even without the apricot tie."

"Joking aside Denny, I am a desperate man," his face assuming the role.

After a pause in which Denny thoughtfully rolled a third, yet unlit, cigarette between his thumb and fore-finger, he said, "Tell me Allen. If I had a sure-fire cure for your malaise, would you take it, no questions asked? Would you let me be your physician, your nurse, even though admittedly I am not tailored for the part? Would you be willing to take some strong medicine adminis-tered by my hand?"

"If it would alleviate this depression I would take a bullet administered by that hand."

"I hadn't anything so gauche in mind," said Denny with a melancholy smile. "What you need to do is to get yourself out of that robe, and into a decent summer suit. Then we can apply the antidote. . . . And please, don't forget to shave. Your cheeks look like a coal miner's."

Allen appeared thirty minutes later dressed in a double-breasted silk suit of extreme burgundy, with lemon pin-stripes. A pomegranate cravat was wrapped boldly around his neck.

Denny led him by the elbow, as one would a sick patient, out of the house, down the numerous front steps, and into the passenger seat of his car.

"Where are you taking me?" Allen asked in a quavering voice. "I hope it's not some kind of home for the uncontrollably eccentric.You know how much I hate to be around sick people."

"We are going to my house," said Denny.

And they drove, under the soft afternoon sun of late summer; into the city; to Denny's brownstone.

. . . Pellington had been at work all that day, under previous instruction from his new employer. Allen was reluctant at first to even sit at the dining table, but after a rather potent sour sop daiquiri, which Denny pushed on him with a grave and doctoral mien, he acquiesced.

The meal was simple, elegant and unparalleled. Red salmon roe and plantain fritters, a baby corn and conch salad, and, for the main dish, a lovely peacock Rouennaise.

It was eaten in silence, Denny glancing stealthily at the other man. He was glad to see that nourishment was being taken, but uncertain of the ultimate results. Since all things are possible, it was possible that Allen could, even after dining sumptuously, return to his ascetic ways. Were he to do so, Denny pondered, a slice of fritter at the tip of his fork, then all hope would be lost. The flavour of the peacock was too extraordinary to leave his mind in any doubt on that score.

Three quarters of an hour later Allen arose from the meal, a freshly brought cappuccino spiked with Dumante in one hand. Sipping the foam from the rim of the cup, he strode over to the window. The city street below was quiet. The house was in an excellent neighbourhood. A middle-aged man in tight slacks walked by. From across the way came the faint sound of music; the jazz of Dave Brubeck. . . . Allen could see his reflection in the pane of glass before him; far from perfectly, but well enough. The feature appearing prominent was his untrimmed moustache. He could see it arching below his nose, crescentic, serrated and strangely exaggerated in the mirror of glass.

He wiped the bits of foam that clung to it away with his bottom lip and then, turning to Denny, said, "It is time to give this slip of hair stuck to my muzzle a trim; don't you think?"

"It might not hurt," Denny replied blandly. "A quick run over with the scissors would not be entirely uncalled for."

"Yes," said Allen, a speck of scintillation appearing in each eye, "I might even consider shaving the whole shag off. I am about due for a makeover."

Brother of the Holy Ghost

"No! Impossible," he said, clawing at his cheeks (lean, gauged, as from hunger, suffering) and then rubbing his eyes.

"It is true though. You have been elected by a unanimous vote of the conclave."

"Ludicrous!"

"Do you accept your canonical election as supreme pontiff?"

He threw his head to the dust.

[*An lxxx year old man kneading his face in the dirt (having fretted himself emaciate for xl years so the devil would not catch him idle—tempting pleading the titter, not merely grilled with hot condiments, but the actual Father of Falsehoods); twisting like a worm, crying like a donkey; an lxxx year old man kneading his face in the dirt, displaying himself grossly, as is all too often the case with the class we call: Saintly Anchorites.*]

This man, very thin, gnarled of face, was named Pietro di Murrone. He ate, once a week, on Sundays, a meal of dried bread and water. He never drank wine or ate meat. *Ora et Labora.* His cell, his chamber, was slightly larger than a coffin; (a living tomb). He wore a suit of knotted hair-cloth bound around the waist with a chain. About his loins, he wore a leather girdle. He shaved once per year, on the anniversary of the Resurrection of Christ Jesus. He had many followers, imitators who were often fanatical, even more so than himself.

July, 1294:

He threw his head to the dust and wept prayers to the being whom he regarded as having power over nature, as well as control over human affairs. The three dignitaries stood by, impatiently, along with a great number of monks and peasants from the surrounding hills.

The question was repeated:

"Do you accept your canonical election as supreme pontiff?"

The old man, Pietro di Murrone, lifted up his head, blinked and looked around him. His eyes were glassy, his lips pressed tight together.

There was a moment of silence
and all options open;
neglected.

He opened his mouth and, showing two incomplete rows of black teeth, said, "Yes," believing   *I have lain down and overcome the temptation   naked. fire   hungry I have foregone sumptuous the feast hot. meat   Bishop of Rome & Archbishop of Roman Province & Successor of St. Peter & Chief Pastor the Entire Church & Patriarch of Western Church & Vicar of Christ Upon Earth   a tree & am little pine tree.*

The dignitaries smiled condescendingly, slyly. The people cheered. Pietro stood, almost stupid.

In August, he received the crown: King Charles and his effeminate son Martel, the King of Hungary, led the old man into L'Aquila on a donkey. The women of the city stood by, in their coarse, tight-fitting dresses and squirrel-lined hoods, sweating and letting out a stench. The men, though gazing with less rapture, did look on respectfully, hopefully. (King Charles had imposed a tax, a penalty on the citizens of L'Aquila of two-thousand ounces of gold; the *boni hommeni*, the gentlemen of the town, had asked Pietro to see what arrangements he could make in their favour.) Though they were hard and accustomed to much misery, they had a certain jaunty bearing. For the most part, the people were without manners or education. Pietro, prior to his coronation, convinced the king to have this tax, this penalty of two thousand ounces of gold, annulled. His wish was granted. Pietro was made pope.

It would be
difficult indeed;—wrenched from a   tattered womb
in a single lifetime   (a solitary hazy green instant)
to compose blunders so many
as Pietro carried out
in those v short months;—dull sorrow and pressed   on
course.

creating, on that xviii day of September, xii fresh cardinals, vii of whom dined regularly on the legs of frogs;—setting the stage for the schism; Avignon. Then: angering swishing cardinals;—reinstating the laws of Gregory X;—suspending the suspensions of Adrian V;— giving privileges ubiquitously;—bestowing the same privileges twice; thrice; iiii times, to completely contrary parties. —While the entire world of Catholic officials shuddered at his gross mis-management of affairs, the old man had a small hermit's cell (slightly larger than a coffin; a living tomb), built in the Castel Nuovo.

"Oh, the peace of a cell," he smiled simply, believing *subdue fearful drops keep it cool   I am fig a latter-day fig   a conclusive desert bloom and the successor of St. Peter Patriarch of the Western Church   I am a little pine tree.*

One thing was certain: He was an easy fellow to manipulate, and Cardinal Gaetani (the future Bonifice VIII) convinced him to resign *ad perpetuam rei memoriam.*

King Charles prepared an opposition. A huge procession of clerics and monks surrounded the castle. They cried tears by the spoonful, prayed, and besought the pope not to let the triple crown tumble, not to abdicate. The *Te Deum* was chanted, with appropriate gusto. But, though he wavered, Pietro was decided[ly uncertain; thoroughly twistable].

Primo: He removed the papal ornaments and clothes.

Secondo: He put on his old suit of knotted goat hair, wrapping the chain around his waist.

"Ah, finally," he murmured happily as he nestled into the garment. "That silk was much too soft and clean."

Nine days later Benedetto Gaetani was proclaimed Pope as Boniface VIII. He cancelled all his predecessor's official acts and took him to Rome. Pietro escaped. He longed for his hermit's cell and made his way back to the Abruzzi.

He had often dreamed   *stop*

[*That abstemiousness, from relative youth to the state of old age, undoubtedly was the cause of some nervous disorder, due to no healthy outlet for fully enacting those higher erotic ends—the real world;— though what filth he laid up in heaven, an angelic auto-erotic dreamland, a firmament of introversion, can only be guessed. For immature childish sexuality (a supremely enticing BVM) often persists into an adult stage of development and results in anxiety-neurosis presenting a picture of sexual excitation transposed into a non-sexual shape of a supremely mischievous nature: the doubting St. Thomas sticking his hand into the wound   crucifixion. spires. baptismal fluid   hands pressed in prayer.*]

He had often dreamed, in previous times, of a tunnel leading   *stop*

naked. meat   & rarest of saints

in early life a

stage of bursting

organic expansion

all the natural impulses

had full play, temptation not leaking out the slightest (those pearly and fearful drops, wicked emission of the human body) well over L years continence must be beneficial I would think, harmlessly keeping it cool   what have I improve my own breed—and me

*(a spineless old fellow certainly) making the great
refusal   Vicar of Christ upon earth   I was was   am fig
now   am flower in desert   withering those withering*
sexual glands
(retained)
excretions [of primary reproductive importance]
[internal] secretions,—glandular
[organism] brain. throat. abdomen
haircloth. chain [thyroid and adrenals]
stimulate. inhibit. rocks. knots
fermentative secretions

   *no temptation is so potent then, so ever devilishly
doing that solitary sexual indulgence*
   but.

cowardice, which he did often wonder about, while,
scampering through woods and over mountains, dexterously avoiding Bonifice's henchmen. He slept in bushes
and caves and prowled up to cottages to ask for bread,
though he lived for the most part off bruised herbs.
While walking through the countryside, he spotted a
dove alight on the branch of a somewhat distant tree.
He sighed; a sound (indicative of longing) that could
be heard. The dove fell to the earth. He approached,
but found a boy there first, ripping out the breasts of
the bird to roast upon a fire. The boy offered to share
his meal. The old man ranted and then lit off into the
forest. He determined to go to Greece, so he made his
way to the coast, just above Venice. He stole into a fish-
ing boat, and pushed himself out to sea, the Adriatic.
A storm blew him back; he was arrested at the base of

Mt. Gargano and imprisoned near Anagni, in a cell stop.

Pietro, Pietro stop. he had often dreamed stop. a tunnel leading to the nunnery stop. arrested at the base of Mt. Gargano and imprisoned near Anagni, in the tower of the Fumone Castle stop.

fire

stop. in a cell. stop. he told himself stop.

"Pietro, Pietro," he told himself. "So, you wanted a cell, Pietro; and a cell you have." In the Fumone Castle stop. in the Fumone Castle. had often dreamed, in previous times, of a tunnel leading to the nunnery. He had often dreamed of a tunnel leading from his cell to a nunnery. The stocks would be blended and the produce disposed of in the garden. (Removing some stones, the tunnel led down and under; out of his cell; and he went through it—the walls were damp and sordid; a sweating unhealthy tunnel.

He went through it to the bevy of them which he undressed; him mad for that he had so longed for:

let the children be buried in the garden: let the children be buried in the garden

taste the white f.t

the white f.t fl.sh

the wh.t. fl.sh .f n.ns

mad and glorious without end be done the rutting done. as long as could rut. as long as could rut

sweating deeper. He probed deeper into the tunnel, its walls sweating fire and *tore their garb threw me upon f.t wh.t. n.ked* n.ked. forms filled them time and again a mad skinny filled them time and again a mad skinny, rutting skinny filled them little beast

buried in the garden: let the children be buried buried in the garden and their bodies be

bit stop. the blue bottles bit, that naked being (slab of sensation), wounded his face to raw sores, pus and blood mixing with tears, which streamed, striped down, forming pools at his feet, attracting schools of repulsive, hungry worms; the punishment (striking vendetta) for those enemies, the cowards, who repulsed responsibility, a narrow breed of gross selfishness

buried in the garden and their bodies be food for worms.)

He fasted and prayed for nine months in this prison, and then died. He was the first pontiff to abdicate.

He was buried in the church of St. Agatha, at Ferentino, but, several years later, his relics were purloined and brought to the city of L'Aquila. His bones currently lie in the Church of St. Maria di Collemaggio.

Dante, in his *Inferno*, situated Pietro di Marone at the gates of hell.

fire

Maledict Michela

I.

A bloated flap of yellow fat hung beneath her jaw; nose: sharp as a cutlass; her eyes were like two shards of shattered sky; she had magnificent ankles. The music blew against her face. She felt the claws of the violins, as they scratched at her old cheeks and thighs, the former pale, powdered, the latter: enormous: like those of a thick-skinned, perissodactyl mammal.

It was on the Piazza Santo Spirito, in Florence, and the Chiesa di Santo Spirito, that final creation of Brunelleschi, rose up behind the scene, a simple geometric façade, of a yellowish-brown colour, like the hide of a sheep exposed to sun and open air.

She, Michela Spadavecchia, gazed directly at the two-toned musicians on the stage. She did not look to her right or left, because she did not need to;—it was certain the people were melting away around her, as they always did, as if her person were some great mass of reeking filth. But she smelled penetratingly of patchouli (sweet as a blossom);—and her looks were not really so much more grotesque than others on the piazza (papier-mâché faces, landscape of fleshy physical structures): young men with untidy hair and endowed with the hips of women, themselves looking as sickly as the pigeons that perched on the fountain; a French female with the countenance of an Eskimo dog; lascivious Italian men, small as crickets; other women, with noses like potatoes, or nests of appalling false carrot-coloured hair resting atop tiny, deficient heads . . .

The G string on one of the violas broke. The conductor clasped his baton,—clasping his baton, he took a step back, lost his footing and dropped his baton. Looks of embarrassment.

She rose up and, with short, slow steps, clicking of two-inch stacked heels, walked over the grease-stained stones towards the statue of Cosimo Ridolfi, to the Via Sant'Agostino, and there turned left.

II.

When young, she had been beautiful; and had been the destruction of many men. Under her care their wells had run dry.

At nineteen she looked like Bronzino's portrait of Lucrezia Panciatichi: a long white neck, a sweet-proud chin and reddish-golden-brown hair. She had known a young man; ignorant, had treated him like a god while he smiled pigs at her, handed her bouquets; she giving to him her flower,—madly in love with him, constantly repeating words of endearment, sweet whispers and bubbling phrases. Then: even when not in his presence she began to repeat his name to herself silently, as if it were some sort of sacred formula. She was obsessed; while he regarded her quite casually;—yet her fire fed on his indifference as if it were fuel; she constantly visualised his face and, unreasonably, feared for his safety. . . . And this caused a strange reaction, even a variety of supernatural reaction formation. . . . As when a plum, left by itself, will dry into a sweet prune, but when a pile of plums are set together for a time, will rot and produce mould and awful smells. . . . In her mind's eye she saw him: drop from ladders, drown in rivers, receive mortal knife wounds.

"I love him, I love him," she would murmur: "Hurt him, hurt him!"

So was her love strangely turned into a negative force; and her eyes, which were the portal for her feelings of affection, cast on him their blight:

1) He became introverted and impotent. Their relations turned to dust.
2) Her second fellow was killed in a hunting accident.
3) Her third was converted into one wholly lacking in amorous power.
4) Her fourth threw himself from the roof of a multi-storied building.
5) Her fifth occurred like her third.

The breasts of mothers, under her admiring gaze, sputtered out only the feeblest drops of milk; and fruit trees became barren.

III.

She took the Via del Monte alle Croci, slowly ascended the steps to San Salvatore, where she sat for thirty minutes in silent meditation. She then rose, issued out the door near the Chapel of the Neri Family, and made her way to San Miniato al Monte. She looked out over the city: the great Duomo, the Campanile of Giotto, and the tower of the Castello Vecchio, as well as the domes of all the minor churches, all this set against a strip of grey, and she felt as if placed in the heights of Domenico di Michelino's famous painting, a mixture of beauty and hell beneath her.

She looked to her right and saw a fragile male figure; the man's gaze however not resting on the view, but on herself, cap-à-pie, feet encased in camel-coloured whipstitched lace-up pumps, vaguely evocative of: desert seductions, woman as captive, love hot and juicy as lamb roasting on a spit: and on such fantasy his mind pitched its tent, her a golden bezel in which he would lodge his over-ripe red heart, the primal predatory instinct to seek out the lame and weakened invoked by her heels.

The next time she saw him, it was from her own balcony. He stood in the window of the hotel across the street and bowed his head. She responded with a smile and returned inside. For two days in a row the same act was repeated. On the third day she received a letter:

Dear and Respectable Madam,

You have, through your smile and the flash of your eyes, charmed me, a guest in room 214 of the Hotel Leonardo. I am not stalking you. I am a mature and lonely man, and I am in love with you. This undoubtedly sounds ridiculous, but it is none the less true. When I saw you for the first time, my heart was thrilled. I crave you, every inch of you, and want to touch your body and listen to the whispers of your soul. I am having spasms for you. Please be so kind as to reply.

Yours Affectionately,

Karl Schrimpf

She replied:

Dear Mr. Schrimpf

I have seen you and you interest me. Tomorrow evening I will be expecting you. Call on me at 8.

Michela

The next evening he arrived at her door at the appointed time: a man with perfectly tended white hair, an extremely delicate upper lip and eyes the colour of kale. He held a potted orchid in the crook of his arm.

"Michela," he said matter-of-factly, with a strong German accent.

"Yes," she replied. "Please come in."

He took a few unsteady steps forward and handed her the orchid. She took it and gazed at the strange pink blossom. It seemed to her that it was something obscene, those flesh-coloured petals emitting an almost sickeningly strong aroma, vanillic, connubial.

IV.

The horizon became pink with the death of the sun.

They ate at Aquacotta. There were crostini toscani and a bottle of Chianti. Karl tried the restaurant's famous egg and vegetable soup and seemed well satisfied.

They walked into the night, along Borgo Pinti and the Via Della Colonna. In the Piazza della Santissima Annunziata he took her hand. The sky was populated with stars. He looked up at the façade of the Ospedale Degli Innocenti, at the small and colourful tondi, sculptures of babies by Andrea della Robbia.

"How charming," the German said.

Michela smiled thinly.

They moved past Giambologna's Equestrian Sculpture of Ferdinand I and onto the Via Dei Servi, Karl humming to himself an aria from Gounod's *Faust*. They passed the Duomo, were in the nucleus of the town, and entered the Via Dei Calzaiuoli.

"Ah, there's a lovely pair."

The two now stood in front of a shoe store, gazing at the window display: pink suede, open toe, heels which were spiked, sharp as daggers. He plunged his fingers in her hair, pressed his desiccated lips to hers.

And so he courted her; the orchid withered and died; manhood for him consisted of spending money, at restaurants, on feminine footwear, of which he was an expert, keeping track of the trends, taking great pleasure in studying the newspaper advertisements. strongly excited: envisioning shoeing her, nailing horseshoes to her feet. That she was far from pretty did not seem to matter, for he saw her not as a woman, but as a shoe, her skin leather, her arms straps, her buttocks and legs a great heel. —And she allowed him to touch her ankles.

V.

His bizarre infatuation with Michela ended in matrimony; a rapid ceremony at San Salvatore.

He repaired to his native land and several weeks later she joined him, took a train to Köln, through Switzerland, through vast mountains and idyllic meadows; then arrived in the city, the rolling stock gliding into its centre (the dual spires of the great cathedral rising up to one side) and into the station.

He greeted her with a kiss on the cheek, loaded her and the accompanying valises into a Mercedes, and drove to his dwelling some short ways into the country. The house looked like a huge coffin. That night they drank champagne; *her foot in his mouth*.

VI.

The lights of the house and the heavy metal shutters on the windows were attached to timers. When the sun set the lights would flicker on, the heavy metal shutters whirr shut. The walls were covered with pictures of horses, as well as photos of Karl, in years gone by, on horseback. He could not ride anymore, but every Saturday would still go to his country club and visit the stables, and with jealous eyes watch younger equestrians enjoy themselves.

He owned a company which manufactured toilet appurtenances. Files, pincers and claw tweezers. Barrel spring toe-nail nippers, gold-handled scissors in the shape of storks, moustache scissors of nickel-free stain-less steel and scissors with micro-serrated edges.

She was soon informed of her conjugal duties: pro-vision the house and serve Karl his supper as well as breakfast and lunch on weekends.

The weather was very warm and they sat outside, under the eaves of the porch. They sipped champagne, Karl ate his daily slice of cake. He wielded a giant orange fly swatter, and with it killed the wasps that came along hunting for food, swatted them and then flicked their corpses off the table and onto the ground, crying out with satisfaction at these little victories.

And then he would talk, his kale-coloured eyes glistening, his speech saturated with stale propaganda: *sacrifice. fight for food. immigration crisis.*

"They say that one day white people will become a minority."

"They say?"

"I read it in a certain book." He looked at her defiantly. "The whites will be slaves. . . . The Africans, you see them coming over now by the boatload. . . . The women with empty bellies and full wombs. . . . The men know how to rob us. . . . And in the future we will be their slaves." He was a visionary, a prophet. "We will be crushed. All this will one day belong to the black man," he said with a sweeping gesture, indicating not only his home, his Germany, but the vast expanse of Europe. . . .

He had been through, survived the war, and though he seldom talked about that part of his life, occasionally he would drop a few words . . . about the Russian front . . . where he had been an artillery commander . . . men freezing . . . living on a pocketful of peanuts.

VII.

The *putzfrau* was a square-shouldered blonde with haunches like a draft animal, fleshy lips and a vague odour of prosaic sin hanging about her person: edacity, frotteurism and evil concupiscence. Five days a week she would arrive in the morning and, after setting before Herr Schrimpf his breakfast, begin disinfecting and cleaning the house. She dusted surfaces and polished all wood, vacuumed and waxed the floors, her large rump thrust in the air and her small nine-volt radio playing, grinding out caricatures of music.

Though she treated Karl with great deference, she was insolent towards his bride, showing all the contempt of the northerner, of one of Teutonic race, towards the Latin, the fryer of fish and eater of cloves of garlic. She muttered darkly under her breath as she cleaned Michela's toilet; then would glide by Karl, graze him with the protruding mass of her breasts, for him turn her frigid frown upside down. . . . And his eyes, those of a very old altocalciphiliac, wandered down to the terminal parts of her legs.

To Michela's extreme displeasure, her husband began to buy the cleaning woman gifts, *id est* shoes: cone heels and fantasy pumps. Their click, the squeak of their leather could be heard about the house interminably, cruel and pedestrian—acousticophiliatically comforting to Karl: *vision of his fleshy, movable, muscular organ (principal organ of taste) wrapped around the solid built-up base at the back of the footwear.*

Michela shrugged her shoulders. She knew too well of his slug-like ability. She was unhappy. She found a kitten for herself, but it drowned; planted tulips, but they were killed by malicious nematodes. Friends? The good folks of the neighbourhood stayed away from her as from some pit so deep it appeared bottomless.

And he: would spend much of his time in moody silences, a nervous twitch distorting his mouth; or, shut up in his room, avidly inhaling the smell of leather.

One night she served pickled herring for dinner.

"Ah, the food of the poor!" he cried in disgust.

The flap of yellow fat beneath her jaw trembled.

"You don't like what I serve you?" she asked with forced calm.

"I like to be treated well."

"How do you treat me?"

"I am a good man!"

"And that is why I love you," she hissed.

His face assumed an expression of mild amusement. He wanted to have the pleasure of seeing her cry.

"If you were not my wife, I would call you a bitch."

Loathing. He was schooling her in how to hate. That night she dreamed of slitting open his belly: her hand, like a great spider, scurried forward and entered the wound.

VIII.

His tread became firmer, his appetite increased. At dinner, instead of his customary quarter litre glasses of beer, he would now drink a full stein; and, with an arrogant accent to his voice, demand a second portion of meat.

One day she heard the sound of suppressed laughter. Bed springs squeaking in pain. Opened door. Starch-white thighs.

His face glowed. His hair seemed more lustrous. His figure acquired a certain robustness, vaguely pubescent,—and this burgeoning made her hate him all the more, though she smothered this emotion with increased outward signs of wifely solicitude. One night she climbed into his bed, found him embracing a pair of thigh-high boots.

"I love you so much Karl," she murmured. Her keenest wish was to see him grilled alive. She now not only dreamed, but consciously desired to see him suffer unpleasantly. She would have willingly scooped out his eyes, torn out his tongue, pressed him in some horrible instrument until his bones cracked and he belched out cries of exquisite pain, his body reduced to jelly.

And then, on a certain Saturday in August, while at the stables, he ventured upon the back of a horse;—and was exceedingly pleased as he made it prance around the corral.

"Karl, you once pledged me your life as a loving and faithful husband."

"Yes."

"You lied."

"Lied?" he snorted. "It was not a lie, only a terminological inexactitude."

He prospered. He walked around the yard barefoot. She despised him. Her walled-up spite was for him the very fountain of youth.

The Life of Captain Gareth Caernarvon

I.

1894. An hour after dawn. Montana. Forest. A large animal, of the deer family. High, humped shoulders. Enormous palmate antlers. It goes down to the edge of the stream, inclines its head, drinks water. A loud, sudden explosive noise. The creature reels off to one side, falls. Eyes wide. Blood runs from a large hole in its side.

Caernarvon emerges from the bushes, dressed in green, his hat decorated with green sprigs, a leafy branch. A moment later a second man shows himself, carrying a Scovill Waterbury camera with a Darlot wide-angle lens mounted on a tripod.

Caernarvon inspects the kill.

The photographer silently arranges the camera.

The hunter takes a pipe from his pocket: the carved head of an Indian chief. Stem in mouth. Smoke upcurling. Beneath the shade of Douglas firs: he puts one booted foot on the belly of the animal, puts the butt of his rifle, barrel upraised, against the thigh of the same leg.

"Shoot," he says. "Take the damned photo!"

A sudden burst of bright and artificial light thrown briefly on the subject during exposure: momentary illumination.

————

From an American picture book:
Fig. 19
June 14, 1894, Red Lodge, Montana
The captain pulling out the heart of a grizzly bear.

Fig. 20
July 3, 1894, Hayden Valley, Wyoming
The captain standing near a pile of buffalo heads. Before his arrival only about 750 bison were known to exist on the continent; afterwards the number was about 550.

Fig. 21
September 20, 1894, Santa Fe, New Mexico
Caernarvon [*broad grin / drunk on blood*] harvesting a javelina.

Fig. 22
November 5, 1894, Orlando, Florida
The captain squatting on head of monster alligator (16 feet and 7 inches from end to end).

II.

As a child, he was absurdly fond of killing insects—ants, beetles, butterflies—practically any little living thing that came within range of his heel, swatting distance of his hand. His favourite book was the Duke of York's *Maystre of Game*, which he would pore over in the evenings, reading of tuskes above ben lowe and ywered off þe nether tuskes it is a tokne of a grete Boor. Young Caernarvon liked to skewer moths on pins, and set lizards on fire. Later, he fished, for chubs, with gilt-tailed worms for river trout. He hunted frogs with a long, spiked stick, or sometimes baited them with gall of goat, and then, like a French peasant, he would roast their legs over a fire of twigs. He took down doves, with his slingshot; and after ripping out their breasts with his bare hands, threw the still warm carcasses to his dogs. At the age of twelve he received his first gun, an E. M. Reilly muzzle-loading hammer gun, and with it shot a pair of fine deer, and blew out the brains of several heads of grazing cattle. As a punishment for the latter offence his father made him wear girls' underclothing beneath his knickerbockers and jacket.

III.

Strong body. Tremendous voice. Determined sunburnt florid face. He had a huge moustache which jutted out from beneath his nose, reclining on thick lips. He looked like a bull elephant in rut. He was an excellent boxer and swordsman. He enjoyed running men through and shooting them in duels.

He duelled a neighbouring landlord, a certain Thornton, who had shot one of his dogs: Early morning. Grass covered with dew. They met in a birch forest, each man accompanied by his seconds. A surgeon was in attendance. Weapon: swords.

Counters and double counters. Caernarvon had a long arm. Straight thrust. Parry in *tierce*. Opponent remarkably cunning in fence, had spent a good deal of time in France. Disengagement. Coupé to the neighbour's neck. Excited at the sight of blood, the captain made a vigorous and somewhat premature assault. His sword flew out of his hand. The landlord, grinning, leapt forward. Caernarvon stepped back, drew a pistol from his pocket.

"A pistol?" said his enemy. "We were supposed to fight with swords. I did not bring my pistol!"

"So much the worse for you," the captain said. "You ought not to have been such a damned idiot as to have left it at home."

And with those words he killed him, terminating the fight.

"Pistols are not to be used except by mutual consent," declared one of Thornton's seconds.

———

Bizarre duels:

Knives strapped to foreheads: men peck like birds, gouge each other in a ridiculous spectacle.

A duel with antique cannons (two 12 pdrs. cast by Perrier Frères) / frightful noise.

. . . got up as gladiators . . . . . .

IV.

1) He married, a woman (Emma) a decent bit older than himself, of money.

2) Said Reginald Wroth, referring to their time spent together in the Congo: "Though he took great pleasure in blood sport, he never did join the rest of us when we went raping the natives. Loved his Emma too much for that I suppose. . . . Yes, he was an . . . honourable man."

3) His fox hunts were some of the best in the country. He would dress the creatures up in outrageous costumes, sometimes as politicians or ladies, sometimes as monks, once or twice as the very pope.

4) Emma was a small woman. Yellow. She was a small woman. Her skin was yellowish.

5) On his estate he caught a poacher, a peasant who had killed a prime stag, and he had the man sewn up in the skin of the animal,

and torn to pieces by his pack of hounds made savage by being starved for seventy-two hours.

6) He had a wonderful collection of hunting dogs: basset hounds; a pair of Wirehaired Pointing Griffons purchased from the Dutch breeder E. K. Korthals; Hungarian Vizslas, golden-red and silky; an Alpine Dachsbracke, short-legged and sturdy, which he had received as a gift from Crown Prince Rudolf of Habsburg; longhaired pointers, Münsterländers; and Irish water spaniels, with long ears covered with dark curls, and curls covering their eyes.

V.

An Extract from the Memoirs of Captain Gareth Caernarvon

My companion was Sir Bruce Roscommon, who was then still in his early manhood, and had not yet succumbed to those brutal vices which were to blight his later life and have left such a gross stain on his once noble character. We had a bodyguard of thirty camel-men, whom I had armed with Lee Enfield rifles. I myself was carrying a Webley double-action revolver, a Mannlicher rifle and, most importantly, a Marlin .45-70 repeating rifle, weighing about 11 pounds and having a 28-inch octagonal barrel.

For four weeks we travelled at a speed of about twenty miles a day, that being as great a distance as a caravan of fully-loaded camels—each carrying around two-hundred pounds of provisions, tents and general gear—can manage. We crossed an extent of arid country, toiled among cliffs and rocky wastes, and then, entering an area more luxuriant, finally halted at the edge of a natural basin filled with muddy water and surrounded by rank-smelling shrubs.

Isibili-Ikhanda-Umkhobe, the two-headed rhino, had been spotted in that area some months before. The natives looked around themselves with wary reverence and mumbled prayers to their devilish gods. I opened a bottle of Linkwood whisky and offered Roscommon a toast to the kill.

Every morning, after breakfasting on strong black coffee and dried ox meat, we struck out, each in his own direction, in search of the tracks of the giant pachyderm. I was particularly intent on putting to death that thick-skinned, heavily built animal, for I dearly wanted such a head for my collection.

The temperatures were frightful. The thermometer rarely went below 110 Fahrenheit while the sun was up. Though I had not yet seen sign of the beast I was looking for, there was still light game: I killed a Barbary lion, warthogs and wildebeests; so our camp had an abundance of fresh meat and for dinner we had delightful stews and then conversed under the stars over our pipes and cups.

One evening, about three hours before sundown, while making my way through a portion of mimosa forest, I came across the fresh tracks of a rhinoceros as well as, to my delight, a goodly portion of its pungent and smoking spoor. The wind was favourable, blowing toward me from the direction in which the animal was moving; and it was apparent that the three-toed impressions in the earth had been made recently, probably within the last hour. My boots were rubber-soled, the terrain I went over flat and soft, generally padded with thick grasses, excellent ground cover. My gait was noiseless. Slowly, patiently I made my way along. I crept around a thicket and there, in a clearing which opened up before me, stood the great brute, about forty yards away, its magnificent hind quarters proned in my direction. It began to turn and I kneeled. One of its heads was gigantic, its nose capped with an exciting horn, while the other head, which grew out of the former's neck, was small and somewhat sickly looking.

I hastily drew a bead upon its chest, squeezed the trigger and let off a bullet. It was an ugly shot, lodging itself in the quarry's flesh without doing adequate damage, and I felt ashamed. The rhinoceros snorted, rose to its feet and turned towards me, levelling its horns and pawing the earth. Then it came surging forward. My life was in peril. Coolly and quickly I set myself up for another blast; looked along the barrel, took aim at the larger head and fired. The shot was fine. The bullet landed square between its eyes. The beast swerved off, and began to break through the forest. Then its legs weakened and it came crashing to the earth. I approached. The rhino writhed on the ground in agony, hot blood spurting from its wound. The smaller head squealed, let out a bleating whistle, and I drank in its cries of pain, for they were as sweet to me as a cool glass of champagne. I then shoved my gun into the mouth of the smaller head and gave it a coup-de-grace, bits of its brain flying out, regurgitating, and dirtying my pants leg.

Smoothing my moustaches I looked down at the animal. There was some unfortunate damage to the skulls, but I, an admirable taxidermist, would still see them nicely mounted.

That evening Roscommon and myself enjoyed delightful umkhobe steaks, to the dismay of the natives.

V.

"It is a lovely gown."

"Yes, I got it for him when I was last in London," Emma said, and took a sip of her tea.

The velvet curtains cascaded down on either side of the panes of glass, making a pretty frame for: green sward, the captain thereon, in feminine attire: an iridescent, two-piece bronze gown. The bodice had a high detachable collar in cream-coloured silk, as well as a large cream-coloured inset which formed a 'V' from navel to throat. The upper portion of the skirt had horizontal ruching with vertical bands of cloth-covered buttons and eight box-pleats, accented with banding and buttons, gave it fullness as it approached the hemline.

————

He wore a corset, experiencing a most pleasurable sensation in being laced tight.

VI.

Sir Bruce Roscommon, the wrinkled flesh of his face ghastly, livid, sat in the restaurant of the Grand Hôtel du Monde drinking a whisky and water and smoking a cigarette. "Caernarvon had the finest collection of stag antlers existent," he said, in a powerful but muddy voice. "All sorts of precious branches of horn, not only that he had secured with his own gun, but historical pieces as well. . . . A damned fine head of a stag shot by Duchess Magdalen of Saxony during the rutting season of 1656. . . . The beast must have come in close upon six hundredweight. . . . A really exceptional twenty-six pointer, such as few men have had the chance at. . . . Yes, those women of old certainly knew how to bring an animal to grass. . . . I don't know what happened to the collection. . . . I suppose his people had them donated to a museum or something of the sort. . . . Maybe sold at auction for all I know."

Roscommon took a long drink of his whisky and

water. "Caernarvon was an interesting man," he continued. "In my youth I admired him greatly. . . . But we had a falling out about something or other; though I don't quite remember what. . . . I suppose he did not approve of my mode of life. . . . And I was not willing to live by another man's system of honour. . . . It was all a bunch of nonsense really. A stupid sacrifice."

VII.

He sat over his pipe. The floor of his study was covered with exotic animal hides, those of tigers and bears, and heads, marvels of taxidermy (gaping jaws, cold glass eyes), and weapons of all sorts were mounted on the walls: silver-hilted swords, outrageous scimitars, Spanish dirks and Russian Kindjals. A beautiful mace, made by the hands of Diego de Caias. Incredible helmets, in iron, gold and silver, shaped as fish, horrible demons. Gun racks: a combination matchlock and flintlock signed François Duclos; an unusual pneumatic canegun made of black laquered brass with a floral-embossed brass pommel and a hidden pop-out button-trigger; a 12 bore percussion shotgun by John Rigby of Dublin & c. & c.

There was a knock.

"Come in!"

The large oak door, which was flanked by two enormous elephant tusks, opened. It was Emma.

"The dress," she said.

"Yes?"

"I have finished adjusting it."

"Oh!" Caernarvon rose from his chair.

"I set it out on your bed."

"Then I will see." The captain set down his pipe and strode forward.

"Would you like some help trying it on?"

"My dear girl, if I want help I will ask for it," he said and exited.

Emma. I have dreamed so very much.

Head of a Buffalo. Is all she does is dream.

Russian Kindjal. We have all seen it.

Emma. Sigh.

Tiger Skin Rug. Will she weep?

Pistol. Oh, yes. She'll weep.

Head of a Buffalo. No. Her eyes are too small.

[Emma weeps.

Tiger Skin Rug. She's crying.

Russian Kindjal. But I don't see any tears.

Head of a Buffalo. Her eyes are too small.

VIII.

In his lifetime he killed an enormous number of animals, as can be ascertained from his punctiliously kept shooting diary: 1,214 stags (34 of which were twenty points and upward), 2,129 red deer, 4,012 wild boar (985 of which were fourteen points and upward), 19 bears, 214 wolves, 11 beavers, 16 owls, 4 falcons, 2,314 vultures, 54 baboons, 2 marmosets, 1 gibbon, 218 hedgehogs, 415 badgers, 617 otters, 501 alligators, 1,107 crocodiles, 1 bongo, 74 bush pigs, 84 giraffes, 119 roan antelope, & c. & c. & c.

———

. . . dipnets, baskettraps, stonetraps, weirs, hooks and lines, rakes and spears.

*

A bait for catching pout:
2 parts Cheshire cheese
2 parts hog's blood
1 part anise seed
1 part crushed bombardier beetle
2 parts galbanum
1 part balsamic vinegar.

*

He had whaled, sunk his fist into the deep blubber of the beast.

*

Woodsmanship; scouting. He caught animals with baits of meat and smells, by blowing on whistles, appealing to their love instincts and other frauds. (Hear him gobble like a turkey.) In deep-dug pits filled with pointed stakes he caught elephants. Spring-traps for wild pigs; nooses for wild fowl; caltrops to catch the fawn. Ambush and stalking (deductions from a broken twig, from the faintest mark in the sand). When hunting with dogs, he kept a bitch's fecund member in his coat pocket, and this stopped them from barking. Then: BANG! His gun would scream out: blood-flecked branches and blood soaked earth. . . . . . .

. . . . [Lions, leopards, lynxes, panthers] bleating goat as bait bait of beef lungs. . . .

. . . . loved he loved to chew the meat of all creatures: of bears and boars of weasels and all sorts of birds: sparrows, hawks, robins, magpies and storks. The need for meat. The need need man's need for meat blood spurting fountain in screams of ape meat bush lizard chimpanzee bush meat. Two rows of white teeth tear. Bush meat wild cat creatures roasted ribs flesh half burnt half raw meat bush plucking out elephants' embryos eye of jackal stewing pot of hippopotamus rip and dig through pain-bright crimson. He wished to net up the fish from the sea and have dead birds rain from the sky. . . . . . . Sometimes he would, in imitation of the Sioux Indians, don a wolf or other animal skin robe, and quietly sneak up on an animal and kill it kill slaughterous obsession dress in pastels pink gown hose kill snatch life power fire guns cut with knife or skewer with harpoon big fish flying bird then those who slither land those live in prairies those meadows see them crumple under gunblasts collapse down dead lovely kill slaughterous flowers perfume of slaughter music-glory of hunt with bow and arrow he could kill. In Australia he hunted like a bushman, dipping his arrows in beetle poison, euphorbia, snake venom or the reddish-yellow caterpillar called ngwa, prepared into a cardiotoxic poison looking like currant jelly.

IX.

October. Emma stood on the lawn. Sad eyes. She wore a velvet gown. An apple was balanced on her head.

"Stand still!" Caernarvon cried. "We don't want to miss now do we?"

"Yes, dear. I am trying to stay very still."

He held up the Belgian breechloading needlefire target pistol, a Montigny & Fusnot, grasped tight the fluted grip and took aim. Squeeze trigger. PAN!

The gun went off; woman fell to ground.

"Damned lousy shot!" Caernarvon growled.

The apple was undamaged, but Emma had a bullet in her skull. Her soul flew out from her body. It hovered nearby for a moment, observing the form in which she had lived, and the husband with whom she had bedded, and then rushed off to the nearby forest where two deer were rutting. The buck's neck was swollen with lust. Having mounted the creatures semen, the soul of Emma entered the hot womb of the estrous doe. There she stayed warm throughout the winter and later, in June of the following year, was reborn as a fawn. She lived in the forest, eating its grasses, drinking from its cool, melodious brooks, and grew strong and beautiful.

Caernarvon came. Armed as always. In search of meat. She was grazing, chewing grass. When she lifted her head the rifle flashed. The hind fell to the ground, a ball through its brain. Caernarvon approached the downed animal. He removed his coat and rolled up his sleeves. After turning the carcass over on its back with the rump lower than the shoulders, he pulled out his knife and cut the animal's throat, bled it. Then, cutting through the hide, he opened up the body cavity and cut out the lungs and the tender heart. He skinned it while the flesh was still warm and that night enjoyed the venison.

X.

". . . So there was nothing for it but to eat him," Jefferies continued, with a gesture of manly resignation. "Nastiest damned dinner I ever did try."

"That is what you get for eating a Frenchy," Caernarvon said from behind the smoke of his cigar. "I would rather have one good stout Englishman in my larder than a dozen Frenchmen."

Jefferies smiled thinly. After three arduous years in the deepest jungles of South America, he could not help but hope for a bit more respect when retiring to his gentlemen's club for a bit of sanitary relaxation.

The waiter came with a tray on which was set a decanter of whisky and glasses. It was Lieutenant–Colonel Reginald Wroth, of the Royal Marines, who did the honours and handed the drinks around.

Jefferies shrugged his shoulders. "Oh, come now,"

he said. "God created all men alike—and I would think to eat one is as unpleasant as the next."

"One as unpleasant as the next? Why, not in the least. A good piece of English meat is never unpleasant. . . . It was when I was stationed in Egypt, under Sir Garnet Wolsley, that I first tried it. . . . A number of us were stationed at a desert outpost between Qasr al-Farafirah and Sitrah. . . . Though at the time I am actually speaking of, we were only two,—myself and a young corporal by the name of Tub. . . . The rest of the battalion had had some bad luck. . . . Russian roulette and all that sort of thing. . . . Damned game was all the rage back then and I was fortunate enough to routinely come up the winner. . . . The corporal was there because his religious obligations had not permitted him to indulge in games of chance."

"Sounds like a wearisome fellow," a voice murmured from the depths of an armchair.

"Yes," added Wroth, "I remember when I was stationed in India back in '92, we used to play Russian roulette with fireworks—seeing who could hold the things in their mouths till the fuse ran shortest, and it was rather fine fun."

Caernarvon smirked with a hint of disdain, took a drink of his whisky and continued.

"Well, the corporal was not what you would call lively company, but he was a good enough sort with a rifle. . . . When the rebels came I believe he shot the heads off a solid six brace. Disposed of them in a workmanlike manner we did. . . . A spirited enough little party we were having, shooting them from the fortification walls, and I believe we could have kept it up all summer if it we had not unfortunately run out of provisions."

"Didn't you have any biscuits?"

"None."

"Well, that is bloody criminal. It is the army's obligation to provide——"

"Oh, settle down will you! Let's not start hearing any sniping of that sort."

"Yes," added Jefferies calmly. "I would like to hear the rest of the Captain's little tale."

"Well, to cut a long story short—I am a man who needs meat. We had eaten every rat in the place, and there were only two pieces of flesh left: myself and Tub. 'Flip for it will you?' I said;—but he insisted that he would not gamble. So be it. I sawed off his arm with my clasp knife and cauterised the wound with a flaming stick. The limb I roasted over the fire, seasoning it with a little gunpowder. I'll be damned if it wasn't the finest piece of flesh I had eaten since I disembarked at Alexandria. . . . Tub admittedly was a bit pale while dining, and did not seem to relish the meal as well as myself."

XI.

The animals knew that he was their enemy. Elephant mothers cursed him for slaughtering their children and, when he approached, even wolves, with their keen sense of smell, fled away in fear. The serpents often considered how best they might assassinate him. Cobras were sent to plunge their fangs into his thigh, and huge boas to strangle him, but he, like some great king, always seemed to be able to foil their plots.

Rattlesnake. He smashed my brother's skull in with a stick.

Tiger. He is strong and difficult to kill. He shoots my ken and strips us of our skins.

Grouse. When he comes my sisters tremble. I tell them to keep still, but in panic they fly off and come falling to the earth, soft bloodied balls.

Rattlesnake. . . . If I could shoot him full of venom . . .

Tiger. . . . If I could shred him with my claws . . .

Elephant. My tusks could gore him.

Grouse. My grandfather told me that man is most difficult to kill, even for condor or eagle, and prophesied ten-million massacres for our kind.

XII.

New Guinea. Incessant rain. He was there to hunt the tree kangaroo. Bang bang hunting wet but good. And then they came. Some with bone through nose. They lashed him to a pole and carried him off, horizontally, back to their village. Women dressed in banana leaves. The children played with him, jabbed him with sharp sticks, threw stones. The chief wore a necklace of seashells about his throat. When the weather cleared time to eat.

Caernarvon stood upright, naked in the pot, the water now heating from the flames beneath. Beating of drums. Some natives danced monotonously around him, bodies glistening with sweat. Others looked on, tongues dangling from hunger-wet mouths. They ate away his flesh comma gnawed his bones period the chief ate out his brains like a giant poached egg comma while his daughters were given the hands which were very choice to eat period he threw the innards the liver etc. to his vassals comma as one might scraps to a dog three dots and then the muscular parts of his body were given to the village boys so that they could absorb his power.

XIII.

There were different hells. Some were small, no larger than suitcases, and within were crammed tens of thousands of beings, crushed together in a horrible vortex of claustrophobia. Others were vast, millions of miles high and millions wide, their floors covered with razor-sharp blades and walls made of white-hot flame. There were hells in all shapes, some triangular, some in the shape of clovers. Maze-like, hells within hells, a chaos of stairways and tunnels. There were a seemingly infinite number of them, stacked up, jammed together.

Now we see: Emma, as shimmering being. She holds sword aloft. Below her a black shadow, something like an empty black bag. It is Caernarvon. He is descending.

He trods through fiery crimson, past lakes of pain and jungles of sharp shards and spines; now wades through streams of blood and rivers of pus, the banks of which were thick with strands of string-like worms and thickets of maggots. The captain transformed, jaws huge, bristling with aciform fangs and dripping death, slavering blood. His moustaches long shaggy tendrils and his belly, protruding from the jacket of his uniform, a second gaping maw. The sinners, the bad priests, the rich, line up before him: and with a huge sledge hammer he pounds in their skulls, drinks their brains like oysters, rips out their intestines and gorges himself. Some, terrified, manage to scurry away, and these he pursues with an immense meat cleaver, scarcely smaller than himself, which he sends swinging into their backs, splitting his victims down the middle.

A Murderer (as his skull is cracked like a nut). Hhh-hhaaaaggggghhhhh!

A Pair of Devils (dancing off to one side). Pè pèèèèèèè pèèèèèèè!

A ball of stinking jelly rolls in from behind a fountain of flame. It is Roscommon. We can see his face: recognisable though massively distorted features. Caernarvon gurgles with glee. It is always pleasant to meet an old acquaintance when abroad. He reveals a pair of red-hot iron tongs and with these proceeds to pull out Roscommon's tongue. He now dips him into sauce before biting off his head.

[Exeunt.

Molten Rage

I.

Smelted. Molten carrion crucible whirring sound. The machine moved the ladle, an enormous metal bucket, forward on the end of a chain. They guided it with their hands.

"Stop!" the foreman cried.

Two rows of large, cylindrical moulds were lined up on the floor.

Massimo was short, with broad shoulders, a thick neck and the eyes of a villain. He had previously worked at an industrial foundry where they made grey and ductile iron castings, but had been fired;—had often arrived late; insubordination to the tune of alumino-silicates and dedusted stuccos.

Now he worked at Fonderia Artistica Bausani.

He loved to see it as it poured. Copper, 10% tin, trace of zinc. They tipped the ladle. Hot lucent orange mud flowed into the opening of a cylindrical block, filling it until its blazing tongue drooled over the top.

They moved from one to the next, down the line, filling them with the liquid bronze.

"I like fat women."

"The capitalist can live longer without the worker than the worker can live without the capitalist."

"The bodies of those beasts, whose blood is brought into the sanctuary by the high priest for sin, are burned without the camp," said Ugo, the patina man.

Each one spoke his own thoughts, without paying the least attention to what the others had to say.

At 6:30 the work was over.

Massimo got in his car, started the engine and drove.

The foundry was located in one of the ugliest areas in the world—on the outskirts of Milan. Huge factories and industrial complexes dominated the landscape, filled the air with an almost unbearable stink. The roads were strewn with nests of small billboards, the skyline perforated by the hooked necks of machinery cranes. Huge smokestacks rose up into the cement-coloured sky and new, shoddily constructed buildings sprang up from great furrows of upturned earth.

*

It was Friday. He did not want to go back to the lonely squalor of his apartment, so toward the city centre; manipulated his little vehicle through the oozing sludge of traffic: trucks roared by like angry rhinos, coughing out clouds of black diesel smoke, scooters buzzing around them like flies, wind inflated the shirt of a young man, streets a river of strange monsters—great engines encased in husks of metal—slobber black oil over the corrupt pavement and fill the air with their shrieks. Indeed, the entire human race seemed enslaved by an insatiable mechanical hunger—men willing to kill, not only each other, but babies, old men and women, in order to feed these creatures in whose bellies they perched like half-digested herring.

*

Up and down narrow streets, maddening search for two square metres of pavement to leave the heap of rubber and screws, no parking so he did so illegally (he already had plenty of unpaid tickets anyhow).

Feeling hunger, he went and ate fried polenta smothered with meat sauce.

His manners were often raw. He was habitually sulky. Without proper reason, he thought himself superior—even as good as the founder of the Christian religion, though his mother, a cleaning woman of southern origins, was certainly no Madonna.

And then darkness swallowed up the meagre day.

He walked along the streets, gaze lowered, the fingers of his hands sheathed in his pockets, a cigarette protruding from his lips. The sidewalks were congested with people—their tongues clicking against the roofs of their mouths. His eyes dove and soared; he nudged his beak through the rising tide of fully developed but more often adolescent flesh which flushed out onto the roadsides on Friday evenings; bleach-dyed jeans; prematurely corrupt faces.

A hand, tapping on the glass from inside a restaurant, attracted his attention. He approached, stared through the pane of more or less transparent silicates, saw his friend Delio, a poet of odious free verse, a little, unshaven man with large lips who had the shifting, neurotic demeanour of a thief or drug addict. (His writing had an mephitic tang to it, like sewage.)

Massimo went inside. Delio was sitting with another man.

"This is Klaus," he said. "He is German but speaks Italian better than I do!"

Klaus had the beard of a mystic—wispy, pointy— and a thin, long face out of which protruded a huge nose like the beak of a bird of prey. His fingers, which he made constantly apparent with lavish gestures, tapered at the ends, were prehensile, and this added to his attitude of a raptor.

Massimo joined the two men and ordered a beer.

"I was just telling Klaus about my latest project," Delio said. "La Società Delle Poetiche Arrabbiate wants to publish a piece of mine in their yearly calendar."

"Brilliant."

"Yes, my poem begins;
I sucked the lubricant from her plastic eyes
Cut her face in half with my tongue . . ."

"No wonder women are attracted to writers," Klaus murmured as he plunged his fork into the last segment of beefsteak on his plate.

"They are partial to deep men."

"No—like animals," Massimo said, taking a sip of his beer, "they rut according to season."

"Speaking of seasons," said Delio, looking at his watch, "I have to go. There's a Nigerian girl I am supposed to meet in twenty minutes."

Delio left. The waiter came and took Klaus's plate away. Massimo finished his beer and ordered another.

"So Delio is a friend of yours," Klaus said.

"He is an acquaintance."

"You are a poet also?"

"No, I work for a living."

"A worker. Earning his monthly bread."

"Have to eat."

"Yes, but if you become too much part of the system . . ." Klaus poured a thread of wine into his glass. "The hardest working slaves are those who consider themselves free."

"Well, if you want to philosophise . . ."

"I do." He filled the air with nebulous ideas. "First off, you have to accept the social revolution as the end to capitalism. The downfall of the corporations. The machinery of government is controlled by the corporate god. Violence is simply a means—to end the state. The code of established morality is another prison. Morality is injustice. Every day 40,000 children die as a result of poverty. Reform isn't enough. The right to vote is a mockery, serving only to consolidate the power of the corporate entity. Action is required—not just words, but complete destruction. Madman, fanatic. Great thinkers are initially misunderstood. A man must fulfil his individual potential."

"So," Massimo asked, "you belong to some sort of organisation?"

"No. I belong to a tactic."

He lifted his glass of wine to his lips and sipped it carefully, as if it were blood.

Upon parting, Klaus handed Massimo some pamphlets and a scrap of paper on which was scribbled his phone number.

"Call me if you ever want to meet . . . for a coffee," he said.

Massimo arrived back at his car, but it was booted. He shrugged his shoulders and threw his car keys into the gutter. He boarded the subway at Cairoli, took the *Linea Rossa*; looked at faces: distorted, shapeless as clods of earth. The passengers sat hunched on their seats—eyes hollow, lips set tight in tense depression. Yes, Klaus was right. These people were simply slaves of some great corporate entity, an entity which they worshipped without even knowing it. Massimo, under the influence of a subtle egoistic intoxication, felt as if he could knock the human race over with a word, destroy it with a few blows of his fist.

At Amendola two young men got on. One held an accordion, the other a guitar. They began to play, stubbornly, somewhat clumsily. Then the beggar's cup went round. A woman dropped a valueless coin in—and then they debarked, at Lotto. Massimo himself got off a few stops later at Uruguay.

He lived in the Quarto Oggiaro. Sinister activities, homicides, violence of every genre.

On the street, darkness, gliding shadows. He had a good walk, as the stop was far from his home. He passed by a group of Albanian prostitutes. That area of town was full of women either exploited or exploiting themselves. They lurked under the street lamps, flitted along the sidewalks like bats.

Gentle boiling red, painful veins desire sacred whore

submit to sterilized fecundation.

Finally he was there. He made his way through the entrails of the building—up stairs—through halls;—then, arriving at his door, he realised that, when he had thrown away his car keys, he had also thrown away the key to his apartment. He rammed the rectangle of wood with his body, hurt his shoulder, forced the lock.

His apartment had a stale smell. Furniture crammed into two small, high-ceilinged rooms. He threw himself on his bed and slept.

II.

He lived amongst the constant roar of machines, grinding of metal, shouts and spray of sparks. The place was crowded with sculptures in various states; wrecked plaster busts, women abhorrent nudes of bronze, monumental mythological themes and questionable contemporary retro-futurist pieces, post-apocalyptic-tribalism which might make one dream of the mating of invertebrates. Then the wax room: full of red figures, some minute, some gigantic, stuck full of nails—sprues—bizarre—more than vaguely masochistic—many resembling huge humanoid candles.

An artist in a white apron—like those worn by surgeons or dentists—stood atop a chair and worked on the wax of his sculpture—a massive male form, vaguely reminiscent of an elongated toad.

Massimo was touching up a figure of Padre Pio, taking the seams out of the wax.

Ugo came striding in, looking for some tool or other. His grey hair had turned green due to all the cupric nitrate and liver of sulphur he used in giving patinas to the sculptures. Stopping, he gazed with admiration at the piece Massimo was working on.

"Do you like what you see?"

"Ah, Padre Pio . . . he was a real saint. . . . The stigmata you know," Ugo said, showing the palms of his hands. "He had them fresh and bleeding for fifty years!"

"*Stigmata del culo.*"

"Hey don't talk that way!"

"If it wasn't for you religious maniacs we would be living in a paradise."

"If you call the flames of hell a paradise, my dear!"

"Idiot!"

"Filth!"

"*Faccia di merda!*"

"*Ruffiano!*"

"*Faccia da blatta!*"

"*Facciakkkallaa-ah!*"

Ugo thrust his hands against Massimo's chest. The latter bunched his fingers together and began to swing—plunging his fists, one after the other, into Ugo's face. Then both men grappled, hugged each other like frenzied lovers, and flew backwards.

A scream, like that of some wild animal, went up. It was the artist. Ugo and Massimo had bumped into the wax of his sculpture, knocked it over, and it had broken to pieces. The strange, somewhat amphibian head rolled under a table. There were pieces of shoulder, a hand, the giant torso broken in three;—all of this bright red—like body parts after some especially heinous crime.

III.

Unemployed.

Filaments of rain descended from the sky.

New Revolutionary Techniques; The Necessity for Violence; Militant Disobedience. These were the names of the tracts that Klaus had given him, and he read them with ardour, his imagination infused with the smell of smoke, the chaos of crowds and the wailing of sirens. He hated. The emotion pushed itself out from within, like a pus-filled boil, demanded expression—in acts of aggression, violence, burning rage. He wanted to destroy—property, people—taste the pain of industrial society as its flesh was burnt smoking black.

A knock at the door stirred him from his reverie. It was Delio.

"I thought you could use some company."

"Why?"

"Why not!"

Massimo lit a cigarette and began to prepare coffee in a little aluminium espresso pot.

"Last of the coffee," he murmured as he emptied out

the dark-brown, almost black powder.

"Hey, do you want to have some fun?"

"I don't want to visit your Nigerian prostitute if that's what you mean."

"No, I mean this."

He held up a can of gold spray paint.

"What's that for?"

Delio laughed uneasily.

"I see," Massimo said.

The coffee boiled. He poured it into two small, white cups.

"Ah," Delio murmured as he stirred a spoonful of sugar into his espresso, "you act like an anarchist, but really you are full of . . . middle-class prejudices."

"*Che cazzo vai dicendo!*" Massimo blurted.

"OK."

The poet pulled a somewhat dirty looking rag out of his pocket, soaked it full of the paint and held it up to his nose and mouth, inhaling vigorously.

Massimo followed suit. The hiss of the paint can, like a snake;—flit of paranoia aching eyelids peeled back drinking melted fig red scorpion genitals of desert sparks. She. Prototype industrial woman, a golden female oozing out of a can: wrapped herself around his feet, as if in obeisance. And he could feel his body changing, becoming mighty, deified, snorting smoke, blazing eyes rolled back in sphere-shaped head. He glanced at Delio. The latter was transformed into a strange batrachian-like creature with tiny glittering eyes and the quivering antennae of a moth.

Massimo opened the window and began to crawl out.

"Are you crazy!" Delio cried, and flung himself on Massimo's back, clung there, the latter on the sill a vast sweep of molten air before him in aching strange red-gold tumble.

Together strength of deity of drug of hate (through Massimo's power) they began to float out and over the city, which boiled below, he soared above, the air around him hot as fire. Sucked up bodies spewed out ground corpses sprayed city slippery red muck blue steam sooty steam.

A giant serpent was curled up in the clouds.

"I am Tyrrhenian Sea Dragon," it said. "And what deity are you?"

"At the moment Gold Vapour God!"

The next morning Massimo awoke with a terrible headache. He opened his eyes and looked over at the clock, but is seemed incredibly distant, as if it were miles away. His body manipulated itself out of bed, made its way to the kitchen; hands fumbled with the coffee tin. . . . Empty. . . . He pulled on some jeans and left the place, to walk to a café. The streets seemed to be strewn with small pools, red, as if they were pools of blood.

IV.

He began to meet Klaus regularly in town, at the restaurant, and the latter, in his cultured voice, the voice of a professor delivering a lecture, would set forth the philosophy of violence, the working man's revenge on the great corporate machine. Sometimes he would fall into a sudden whisper and then deliver some very specific tit-bit, some morsel of information that his listener might draw on if he wished to make himself useful to the cause. And Massimo, nodding his head gravely, furrowing his brow, smoking cigarette after cigarette, lapped up this revolutionary talk as if it were water and he a thirsty dog. Ah yes! He was all for destruction. Let the whole world burn, so that the brightly-feathered phoenix of the future could rise out of its ashes!

V.

"You are in love?"

"No. She is meat."

Delio had a rash around his nose and mouth. His whole person smelled of solvents.

The two men were in the city centre. They walked past the statue of Vittorio Emanuele II. An African in a huge yellow t-shirt, seated before the rearing heap of cast metal, motioned to Delio, but the latter ignored him. The Duomo, that largest of Gothic cathedrals, was there before them.

"Shall we go in?" Delio asked casually.

"What for?"

"Don't you like churches?

"No. I hate them."

"Ah, it is morbid inside . . . inspiration for poetry."

Through the huge bronze doors. Into the cool interior. The dark forest of the immense stone pillars. The large crucifix suspended about the chancel contained a nail from Christ's cross.

They wandered around, gazed dumbly at the vast stained-glass windows. Massimo's repugnance was mixed with a gloomy fascination. The place was incredibly grand, dreary, filled with the perfume of incense and the flicker of candles—a place where people suffered and murmured mushes of prayers through n-shaped mouths to the god they would never realise.

Then the two men found themselves at the entrance to the staircase which led to the roof. Delio took out his wallet and, with shaking hands, paid the entrance fee.

"Come on, to the top."

Massimo shrugged his shoulders and followed his friend.

They climbed the steps, were soon there, on the roof of that great church looking out over the smoke-stained city. Ranks of spires jutted up hungrily around them, each one dizzily capped by the statue of a saint, the highest of them crowned by the Madonnina, her body coated in gold. Whole quarries of marble had been expended to form this structure of which they stood atop, with no other company than a family of Spanish tourists whose lisps added a disturbing electricity to the environment.

The roof was bordered by a carved stone railing. The city was there, spread out like a map and Massimo, gazing over it, felt the power of a superior being swell up within him.

The family of Spanish tourists left, could be heard laughing, talking loudly as they descended the stairs.

Delio stepped over the railing. "Follow me," he said.

"But why? Are you crazy?"

"It is interesting."

Massimo followed. Up amidst the masses of marble, the expressive stone saints. He looked down, at the flying buttresses and then the piazza, dotted with people, small spots of colour; then splashes of pigeons, which looked like ash dropped from a cigarette. Their position was incredibly precarious; and he did feel a vague sense of satisfaction, like Zeus looking down from Olympus.

"Imagine jumping off of here," Delio said.

"Imagine."

Delio took a pack of Suzy Longs from his pocket, lit one, and then offered the pack to Massimo, but the latter shook his head.

The poet, the paint sniffer, dragged at his cigarette, looking intently at his companion.

"Go on, do it," he said.

"Do what?"

"Fly—like you did before." He had a wild, unsettled look in his eyes, began tugging at Massimo's shirt sleeve, motioning the latter out into the abyss. "Fly."

"Get away from me, or I'll smash you and toss your flimsy body off here."

Ten minutes later they were back on the piazza, both pale and silent. They walked along the Via Torino. Massimo was angry, queasy, disturbed; felt as if he were being watched and looked behind him, at the African in the large shirt, the same who had been seated before the statue, but who was now following them, accompanied by two other men.

The Italians turned onto one of the small side streets that lead indirectly towards the Corso Magenta. The Nigerians advanced rapidly, caught up with them.

"Ciao Bem," Delio murmured.

"Mama said you wouldn't pay Eliza."

"I'm going to pay her."

"She said you were rough with Eliza."

"I wasn't. Not at all."

"Let's see your wallet *ragazzo*."

"There's nothing in it."

"Wallet *ragazzo*. Let's see the wallet."

"Massimo . . ." Delio gurgled.

One of the Nigerians looked at Massimo. "You want trouble?"

Massimo frowned. "No," he said, turned and walked off, in back of him could hear the high-pitched cries of the paint sniffer poet, as the latter was throttled, kicked and finally stabbed.

VI.

He spent his time laying on his bed, smoking cigarettes, envisioning acts of grand destruction: glass flying through the air, fountains of flame roaring skyward. A shrine of beer bottles accumulated in the kitchen. He formed vague plans for poisoning the city's water supply with LSD, for assassinating the prime minister and destroying the seats of government through violent means. His mind floated off, plunged itself into the bowels of the earth where it heard the tortured screams of the damned, gazed on lakes of molten brass and lava. He imagined himself as god, created a mentally-generated body: with dark blue skin, four arms, the head of a camel. He rose into the air and stroked the moon.

After all, even slime-minded Delio had known he had power.

Massimo perceived two selves: the one a man—worm with bones, a piece of red meat garnished with cognitive faculties; the other a being of great strength.

Issuing out onto the street, he saw the citizens not as sentient human beings to be loved and cherished, but as walking skeletons—skeletons covered with so many pounds of flesh, veins filled with so many litres of blood. When a beautiful woman smiled at him, he saw not her plump, cherry-like lips, but her skull filled with a wet and barely functioning brain—of little more value than an oyster in its shell. But what agitated him the most, what made his teeth grind and his armpits sweat, was the sight of rich gentlemen in suits. These he wanted to grind up, blow up, douse with acid, turn to dust. One day he even went so far as to assault one of these gentleman on the street—for no reason—simply in a mood of anguished rage. . . . After pummelling the man for five minutes he turned and stalked off, thinking mountains of bones would not be adequate to satisfy his gnawing hunger.

"The people should worship me," he thought, "offer me garlands of cop flesh. Skewer themselves on giant blades at my feet—for my pleasure. . . . Swallow bombs and let me see them blow themselves to shreds."

Volleys of fury; lashed by amethyst thunder.

VII.

Klaus leaned back in his chair, gravely stroking his beard.

"The static misery of today's electro-mechanical civilization . . . because there is always a surplus population, to be used as fodder for wars—a population which is daily being reduced to the powerful chemico-gelatine which feeds the Machine."

"The question really is what to do."

"The world has to be destroyed before it can be rebuilt."

"We will see. I will go to Genoa."

The German lit a cigarette and gazed, through the window, onto the street, with far away eyes.

VIII.

He wrapped a black bandana around his face and walked with the crowd. Officers, a wall of riot shields banged by batons, advanced down a side street off the Via Giuseppe Casareggi. Clouds of tear gas; bottles hurled in counter-attack. Stun grenades. The panicked shriek savage demolition spat star-shaped forward bricks a stink human vapour tangled joy in wads of angry meat. One man took a pole and shoved it through a window, others smashed up shops, howled like dogs. A woman was seen kneeling by a lamp-post her face buried in her hands. Cars overturned and set to flame amidst howls of frightened and angry glee, paving stones ripped up and tossed at carabinieri.

"*Avanti! Avanti!*"

He hurled a Molotov cocktail at an armoured police transport. It smashed against it, spreading out into a sheet of flame.

Blood-stained pavement, sobs, the patter of running feet.

Next thing he knew he was struck—a massive blow of a truncheon to the back of his head;—grabbed and violently pushed to the asphalt. Two policemen dragged him over railway lines towards a signal box.

"*Sono Dio!*" Massimo screamed. "I am God!"

The officers kicked him and beat him with their batons while he, instinctively, curled up into a foetal position for self-protection. Finally a group of protesters, throwing stones at the police, managed to free him. He stood up, not even fully conscious, his face painted with blood, and stumbled away.

IX.

In Milan. Evicted from his apartment, he squatted in an abandoned building in Gratosoglio, now a creature who lived in dark places, like a centipede. Tired, impoverished, gloomy, he went unshaven, lurked around the train station, that nest of vice and criminal misdeed, magnet for human leeches.

He scratched himself, peeled back his eyelids and gazed at the passers-by: huge maggots wrapped up in cotton, shod in leather, draped in synthetic fibres. He walked, lifting his leaden feet; stared at the ground like a man searching for treasure;—a stinking cigarette butt, some small coin, riches of the gutter.

On the corner of the Via Vittor Pisani and the Via Napo Torriani, that busy intersection at the Piazzale

Duca D'Aosta, he noticed a man waiting for the stop-light. He was well dressed, with the wispy, pointy beard of a mystic.

It was Klaus and he approached him.

"Ah, it's you," the German said. "You look horri-ble—filthy. . . . You must be living outside the capitalist system. Surviving off its refuse like a famished rat." He ran his hand through his beard. "I would join you if I could, but unfortunately I am a political animal. You can eat away at its exterior, I will burrow inside like a worm. . . . Yes, we are both, each in his own way, despised creatures, seeking revenge on the monopolic giants who have chained us."

And his voice, that of the professional lecturer, droned on, vaguely delineating the man's philosophy and morals.

Massimo, who had eaten nothing but garbage for the last three days, had difficulty listening. He felt his stom-ach churn; asked for a handout.

Klaus looked slightly astonished. "Give you money? I am afraid I can't. It is against my principles to give only for the sake of charity. Private property is not yet abolished and . . ."

His words were lost in the roar of a truck engine. The next moment he was waving goodbye and crossing the street.

Massimo shifted his way along the sidewalk; fell into the shade of an alley, removed from his pocket a can of spray paint not yet empty, and proceeded to let the golden girl rape him.

Vishnu had once descended to earth and lived his life contentedly as a pig. Massimo was the new Avatar—drowning in the waste and crime of the city—feeding off filth and drinking industrial piss. God, revolution, love, prosperity: words for him as empty as the monotonous tone of a bell drifting through space.

The Chymical Wedding of Des Esseintes

Holiday was not all it was made out to be and he was no longer a young man and it was difficult for him to find pleasure in tramping about the streets of some foreign city with his nerves grated on at every turn.

Des Esseintes sat wearily in the café, gazing out at the pedestrians as they passed, marvelling at how ugly they were: women like giant lizards strutting about in silk, men with stovepipes balanced on their meagre craniums, children who looked like over-sized rodents and went by nibbling on apples, their eyes darting around suspiciously.

But then, he reasoned, he was no beauty himself, his once handsome face lined with wrinkles, his head bald, his body thin and covered with loose flesh.

He sipped at his glass of slivovitz, knowing very well he was beyond the time when such things could possibly stimulate his mind.

He wished he had been back in Paris, not because he liked the place, but at least there he could exist without effort. Here on the other hand it was all wrong. His digestion had been violently upset for the past three days due to the concoctions of cabbage and old meat he was served up nightly, which he was forced to wash down with some acid beverage the hotel keeper tried to pass off as wine. He had looked over the architecture and tried to keep from yawning, but in the end, the inertia of the man who has seen too much overcame him.

"French?"

Des Esseintes looked over at his questioner, who sat at a table next to him: a small individual with a neat brown beard and large eyes that stared at him from behind spectacles.

"Yes, I suppose so," he said in a tone that did not invite further conversation.

"And do you like our city?" the other persisted.

The Frenchman smiled bitterly. "Like would be a strong word."

"But you have come here."

"Arbitrarily."

"Nothing is arbitrary. The world is guided by karmic principles. Human beings ebb and flow according to the laws of gravitation."

Des Esseintes was silent. He couldn't very well disagree with that. He had exhausted all of life's pleasures many years earlier, but due to some force he himself could not explain still found himself lingering about, waiting without interest for something, though he knew not what.

The man introduced himself. "My name is Harro. Harro Pernath."

Des Esseintes murmured his own name and watched as a waitress deposited a glass of slivovitz in front of the other man, who winked, pulled out a little flask and poured a few thimblefuls of its contents into his drink.

"Ether, sweet vitriol, or, as some call it, the astral light, which mixed with spirit becomes earth. Capricorn and Taurus meet Mercury. The quintessence of matter."

The man began to interest Des Esseintes, who took a swallow of his own drink and observed the other's eyes, which flashed with an odd intelligence. The fellow reminded him vaguely of a Japanese curio he had once had at his house in Fontenay.

"So, you have seen the sights of our city?"

"I suppose so. I have seen what is around me. But . . ."

"But?"

"Nothing. I have not been caught much by the motif."

Pernath looked at him with what seemed to be genuine pity.

"If you wish to be entertained . . ." he suggested.

"I don't."

"When you need food, you make a calf."

"And you know how to make a calf?"

"Well. . . . But, have you ever been to a Prague wedding?"

"No."

"A dear friend of mine . . ."

"They would not mind having a stranger among them?"

"If you are with me, you are no stranger. You will be welcomed, and no doubt impressed, because not everyone can see . . ."

Des Esseintes, though not terribly tempted by the offer, acquiesced, as much out of a sense of boredom as anything else. Anything would be better than going back to his hotel and placing himself in the hands of its cook.

He paid for the drinks; they rose and left the café.

Night had fallen, and a reddish moon had risen up in the sky.

"There are four ways to get there," Pernath said. "The first is short, but unpleasant. The second is quite nice, but takes a long time. The third is really beautiful to go by, but I am not sure you would appreciate it."

There was silence.

"And the fourth?" Des Esseintes asked, without a great deal of curiosity.

"No, better leave the fourth alone," Pernath said hastily.

"Well, you decide."

"I'll take you by the first. It is a bit rough, but we'll get there more quickly."

He pulled the flask of ether out of his pocket and took a swig.

"Go on," he said, handing it to Des Esseintes.

"And why not," the latter murmured, taking the flask and lifting it cautiously to his lips. He felt the beverage slip down his throat, move about in his stomach like a live frog.

They made their way into the Josefov. Des Esseintes had been under the impression that a great portion of the ghetto had been destroyed, but the area they went through seemed vast and there was no evidence whatsoever of rehabilitation.

He was being guided through narrow lanes. Disagreeable looking prostitutes hung their heads out of the windows of sooty dwellings and offered their services in strange tongues but unmistakable terms. Children with intelligent faces walked by and winked and showed mouths of moon-coloured teeth. A man with a beard dripping down to the ground sat at his doorstep constructing human figurines out of clay by the light of six candles. On the doorway behind him, beneath a mezuzot, was a small sign which read:

Here Lives Zambrio, Magician

Des Esseintes looked at his guide questioningly.

"No," Pernath said. "You don't want to be caught up with him."

A dog with a long, thin muzzle walked by and Pernath weaved his arm through that of Des Esseintes and led him on.

They turned down a remarkably narrow alley, which led up a series of steps, which were moist and very slippery. The alley dead-ended abruptly in a high wall in which rested a small door.

Harro Pernath opened the door and the two men stepped into a tavern in which the shapes of men could be discerned amidst great clouds of tobacco smoke.

"This is a shortcut."

They moved through the low tables, around which men were hunched, drinking glasses of brandy, slivovitz and beer; smoking pipes and long cigars. Then along the counter, behind which were ranged beer engines, huge bottles of liquor with Hebrew written on the labels and a table on which sat baskets of bread and three or five cooked cow tongues.

A huge man with broad shoulders and a bristling black moustache came and clapped Pernath on the back, crying out in a language Des Esseintes assumed to be Yiddish.

"This is my cousin Lipotin," Pernath said shyly. "He insists on treating us to a drink."

Before Des Esseintes had time to say anything, a huge tankard of beer was thrust into his hands.

"Drink!" the man said in a guttural tone.

The Frenchman lifted the pecan-brown liquid to his lips and swallowed down a draught, which tasted vaguely of mushrooms, of old earth—of something dug up from the ground. He looked around him, fascinated to some degree by the people he saw. Men who existed behind moustaches the size of brooms and in whose eyes he could see reflections of far off lands. A white-haired gentleman who propped up an enormous black hat with his head. A very intelligent looking woman who sat in a corner, flanked by two stout fellows fondling long knives.

Des Esseintes swallowed down his beer and gave his guide an enquiring look.

"I have to buy a round now," Harro said. "Otherwise

it would be impolite."

Three more tankards of beer made their way into their hands. Lipotin was growing merry, reciting some story in Yiddish, chuckling, showing formidable rows of bay-coloured teeth and continuously taking Des Esseintes by the shoulder and shaking him affectionately.

"He says you remind him of an old girlfriend of his," Pernath said.

"Flattered. But shouldn't we . . ."

"Yes, yes, we can't be late for the wedding. You treat us to a last round and then we'll be on our way."

Des Esseintes was beginning to feel dizzy. But, smiling grimly, he held up three fingers to the barman.

When finally they stepped out the back door, he trod on the tail of some unknown animal which screeched and then bolted off into the darkness.

The two men wandered down narrow lanes, with unsteady steps, until they found themselves in a claustrophobic square with a well in the middle.

Above them were windows, the yellow-painted shutters of which were all closed.

Pernath called up, and the shutters to one of the windows was flung open and a knotted rope let down.

"Up we go," he said, grabbing hold of the rope and, with great ability, climbing to the top and through the window.

"Come, come."

Des Esseintes frowned. He did not feel comfortable engaging in such acrobatics, but in the end did struggle up the rope and through the window.

The room he found himself in was quite large, the walls hung with elaborate tapestries depicting green lions, crescent moons, heavenly birds and golden crowns. A number of large canvasses hung on the walls: one of Yehudah ben Bezalel Levai, another of Ramban.

A very small, very old man who wore an odd-shaped hat the colour of spring onion greeted him.

"We have been expecting you, my child," he said, taking Des Esseintes by the hand and giving him a look of great kindness.

"I have come for the wedding," the other said with some embarrassment.

"Why, of course you have!"

"Let him see the bride," Pernath commented.

"Yes, yes! Let's take him to Vyoma."

The old man gently pulled Des Esseintes by the arm into an adjoining room where a young woman sat on a satin divan staring into space.

She was small and pale. Des Esseintes had a hard time determining whether her face was beautiful or the very opposite. She had a blood-red ribbon wrapped around her throat with the words TEM. NA. F. written on it in purple.

"Maiden's milk," Harro Pernath said slyly and then chuckled, poking his guest in the ribs with his elbow.

The Frenchman was just beginning to mumble some awkward words of admiration when a very fat woman with large ears carrying a pink feather duster came bustling into the chamber shouting.

"Out! Out! You men are always too eager. Better to first purify your hearts!"

She thrust the feather duster at them and the men retreated from the room.

"In time, in time," the old man murmured as he led the others into a small closet and then up a long ladder into a room which was crowded with clocks, a piano, a brass elephant and bric-a-brac. In the middle of the room was a table, covered with food. In one corner, in a large cage which sat atop a marble pedestal, was a curious bird, with yellow feathers and a long neck. A terrarium filled with African mice sat on a shelf.

Crowding the middle of the room was a large oak table on which were piled formidable cheeses and enormous pies; plates of smoked beef and pickled fish; bottles of Szamorodni wine and brightly-tinted liqueurs.

Des Esseintes lit a cigarette and sat down.

A group of musicians burst into the room and, after helping themselves freely to wine, began playing at their instruments violently. Harro jumped over to the piano and started to pound at its keys. A thinnish man with a moustache scraped away vigorously at a violin while another fellow, whose sleepy eyes relaxed behind a pair of spectacles, hammered on a cimbalom. A brooding looking man in his thirties blew on a clarinet.

Des Esseintes tried to follow the rhythm, which reminded him vaguely of certain passages of Christoph Demantius, but in the end gave up and turned his attention to the table.

A sudden hunger had come over him. He cut himself

a huge slice of cheese. There was a bowl of hard-boiled eggs and, peeling the shell off one, he dashed a bit of salt on it and shoved it in his mouth. Then he cut himself a piece of rhubarb pie.

The violinist looked at him and shouted, "Feed the bird."

Everyone took up the theme and all began shouting uproariously for him to feed the bird.

Des Esseintes, tearing a piece off a loaf of bread, took it to the cage and let the bird peck it out of his hand, at which everyone clapped and screamed in delight while the bird began to coo and run around its cage in excitement.

The violinist introduced himself.

"My name is Gustav."

"Yes?"

There was a strange light in the eyes of the musician.

"Do not be so sure."

Des Esseintes was baffled.

"He is talking about the transformation," the clarinet player said in a bored tone. "Complete non-discrimination. It's like last night. I dreamed of a man with huge antlers playing the guitar."

"And how did he play?" asked Gustav.

"Better than you, only I couldn't hear."

"Then how do you know?"

"The same way I know that the bird is happy."

"Don't talk nonsense Alfred," the cimbalom player said. "The bird might be the body, but it's not the blood. The height of feeling leads to the path of God. No question that there is beauty in ugly pictures, but that doesn't mean our French guest here should have to endure the worst. Let him have a glass of wine and be on his way."

"He's here for the wedding," Pernath said.

"We all are!" cried Gustav. "Max is just trying to annoy us. He doesn't like to celebrate. He's waiting to return to the promised land."

"Ah, you occultists . . ."

"Hush, hush!" the old man interposed and then, approaching Des Esseintes, kissed him on both cheeks.

"She's ready now."

"Ready?" the Frenchman asked in astonishment.

"Don't be shy my child. She likes you very much."

"Make sure to kiss her on the lips," Pernath whispered in his ear.

Before he knew it, he was mounting an elegant spiral staircase of brass work.

The room he made his way into was totally round with an imposing bed stationed in its centre. She was lying there, with a blank expression on her face. He moved closer, and opened his eyes wide with surprise.

"Great God, she's——!" he said to himself.

Yes, she was there, a man past his prime, with a balding head, face lined with wrinkles, body thin and covered with loose flesh.

He stood for a moment in indecision as the fellow looked up at him. Reasoning that at least he could not accuse himself of mediocrity, he leaned over and placed his lips to his, fed on his own substance. The figure on the bed, some strange, perverted mirror-image of himself, shrugged its shoulders.

A shiver coursed over Des Esseintes' body and he was considering what course to take when the door to the apartment was flung open and everyone entered in a storm. The musicians were banging on pots and swinging their arms in the air. Harro Pernath carried the caged bird on his head and the old man was dexterously juggling the hard-boiled eggs. The African mice were mounted on Gustav's shoulders.

Everyone sang in unison:

> Now likewise
> He brings joy
> To the nuptial ceremony
> Of D.E.

> All is gladness
> That he is equal
> So the betrothed
> Will multiply.

Des Esseintes' body broke out in a wintry sweat. He began to bite his nails, while the figure on the bed gnawed at his.

"Let me take your jacket," the woman with the large ears said.

"No, no," Des Esseintes murmured as he backed towards the door.

He turned and ran out of the room, down stairways and ladders and then stumbled down some dark steps and through a groaning door.

He found himself outside. The night was chilly, and he pulled his coat around himself.

Looking down, he noticed a dirty-looking girl tugging at his sleeve, putting an empty hand forward. He threw some money at her and moved off, towards his hotel, to pack his trunks and portmanteaux as quickly as possible.

The pleasures of foreign cities certainly were exaggerated, he noted as he hurried on with the elastic steps of a much younger man.

The Search For Savino

written in conjunction with
Forrest Aguirre

I.

My search for Savino began in 1926, while visiting the famous art collector and critic Sir Timothy Broughton. He was a man of ample means. His taste was highly cultivated. Night or day, a bottle of chilled champagne, always quality stuff, was by his side, and for this reason, no less than the pleasure of his conversation, I was apt to call on him frequently.

One day our conversation turned to the subject of great artists who had never got their just deserts. I mentioned Pierre Puvis de Chavannes and Henry van de Velde both as being artists who I thought fell into this rank, both being absurdly neglected considering their skill and the impact they had.

Sir Broughton puffed at his cigar and shook his head knowingly.

"Have you ever heard of Savino?" he asked, with a rather indescribable look in his eyes, something like a magician might have when imparting a secret formula.

I thought for a moment, gently sipping my champagne, and then informed him, with some slight embarrassment, that I had not heard of the man he had mentioned. He rose gravely from his seat and requested me to follow him into his study, which I did with much curiosity. When we reached the room, he pointed to a quadro hanging from the wall. It was obviously a relatively recent acquisition, because I had been in the room several times before and never noticed it—and though not in any way loud, it was a very noticeable bit of work. It was a strange stretched canvas, painted all in blue, a damned haunting shade of the colour, a sort of gloaming tint, full of melancholy. The depiction itself was of a rhinoceros, standing in the midst of a forest of strange letters and symbols. I could not make head or tail of it, but was sure that it was full of some deep meaning, possibly sinister, and I had great trouble dragging my eyes from the piece.

"Is this his work?" I asked, with some emotion.

"Yes. That is Savino. Back of Anthony Wexler you're looking at now."

I did not know what to reply. Sir Broughton calmly lit his pipe and pointed to a stack of papers on his writing table.

"Take a look," he said. "It is a catalogue I'm working on. For Sotheby's and all that sort of thing."

I took up a sheet and read:

Item:

The Property of a Gentleman

For Charon: Two Confederate American gold coins, one obverse on the left eye, one reverse on the right,

tattooed on the eyelids of retired Confederate Colonel Josiah Stoat, Georgia, United States of America. An inscription in black beneath the left coin reads 'For Charon', *inks of ochre and cadmium*
45mm x 13mm and 44mm x 12mm

Item:
From the collection of Prince Georg Lubomirski, Formerly deposited in the Museum at Lemberg, Poland

THE SPICE RIVER: A single dhow, piloted by a richly-dressed oriental merchant (actually a portrait of the client Xhien Xo Pyang) slowly floats down a languid river. The river's water is stained with the hues of cinnamon, cardamom, anise, turmeric, coriander, powdered ginger and peppercorns, *ink of charcoal and mixed spice ink concentrates, right eyelid of the merchant Xhien Xo Pyang.*
39mm x 10mm

Item:
The Property of a Gentleman

HIS LOVER'S EYES: A collage of twenty-three irises and pupils, each image taken from the body of the original. Each eye reflects the face of the client—the much-feared and renowned rapist and serial killer Renault DuChampe—at various ages. Behind this montage is a single large iris of deep brown: that of DuChamp's un-named hangman, *manganese based salt inks, left*

eyelid
   39mm x 10mm

Item:
   *The Property of the late Madame Winifred de Roths-
child*

COPY OF MOORE'S THE EPICUREAN, WITH SEVERAL PAGES
SKETCHED ON BY ENZIO SAVINO, in one volume, printed by
A. & R. Spottiswood, New Street Square 1832, bound in
leather with gold lettering on spine, slight foxing

List of pages on which these drawings appear:
a vi, recto: Slight study of one fat gentleman, *black
chalk*
p. 3: Uncomplimentary study of Ferdinand Keller, *black
chalk*
p. 164: Study of Zeus, *black chalk, touched in pen and
ink*
Three loose pages of blank paper inserted at this place
p. 270: Study after a porphyry sculpture of the emperor
Heliogabalus, *black chalk*
End page: Study of Prometheus saved by Hercules,
black chalk, touched in pen and ink

Item:
   The Property of Mrs. Lisa Stewart, of San Francisco

ROMNISOVIC'S SUPERNOVA; RIGHT EYELID: White stars
superimposed on a light blue grid over a black

background. The single brightest star is named for the client, Sergei Romnisovic, who discovered it in the midst of much public controversy over his private life and heretical religious beliefs, *charcoal and rye inks*
   38mm x 10mm

Item:
   The Property of Mrs. Lisa Stewart, of San Francisco

Romnisovic's Supernova; Left Eyelid: Block-scripted letters and numbers listing information regarding the star:

$$\text{RA (1900): } 15 \quad 41 \quad 47.2$$
$$\text{DECL (1900): } +48 \quad 32 \quad 4$$
$$\text{MAG (A): } -4.27$$

   inks of charcoal and soot
   38mm x 10mm

II.

His victims, his lovers, his comrades, whores he picked from the street and boozing oafs he snatched from the bars: drawn back to his chambers: his dark Berlin studio in that third phase of his career.

At first he used nightshade, hypnoticon, the Sola-num manicon described by Dioscorides, a drachme intermixed with wine. But the results were twice fatal, and getting rid of corpses was an awkward business. He toyed with belladonna, but found it too potent: the victims often sleepy for forty hours and more. So he settled for the fabulous sleeping apple: a concoction made from opium, mandrake, juice of hemlock, the seeds of henbane and a touch of musk. This he rolled into codling sized balls. He needed simply give one to his guest and ask her/him to sniff it, a marvelous incense, which when smelt made the eyes gently close and bound them in unbreakable chains of sleep. Unclothed, naked and resting on their stomachs, and the canvas was ripe:

With water impregnated with salt ammonide, quicklime and the oil of galls, he went to work: painting away with rapid, predatory strokes. The designs initially appeared white, but after drying disappeared altogether from sight, the victim awaking with only a rather red and sore region, mere traces: apply to the skin a mixture of litharge, vinegar and salt and they would reappear, even if a hundred years might expire. (Note Enzio Savino's last will and testament and the instructions held therein.)

III.

From an interview with Graham Lynch, cousin of Anthony Wexler:

We had received a letter from Tony regarding the museum piece and the commission Enzio was to receive from Frau von Bekken, which effectively solidified the couple's financial base for life. A few weeks later, Tony sent us the following:

Berlin, September 3, 1898

Dearest Cousins,

Enzio completed his commission work a week ago—a startling composition depicting the mythical hunter Cibembe and his dog cresting the Usagara mountains just east of the Uhehe region. The Colonial Arts Commission felt strongly that, while Chief Bembele was clearly the source of the ill-fated Mele Mele uprising, his bravery warranted recognition. Thus Enzio was hired to etch this African icon of strength and determination over Bembele's eternally-closed eyelids. His head remains on display at the Berlin National Museum . . .

Their future looked quite bright and we hoped that Enzio might now be able to spend more time with his ailing lover (Tony passed on only two years later), but this was not to be the case. Tony's next letter arrived two weeks later:

Berlin, August 8, 1898

My Dear Graham and family,

Enzio's behaviour has grown odd, to say the least. While I trust his loyalty and love for me—which he expresses nightly—I worry for his mind.

Two nights ago, after staying out considerably later than is usual, he returned home only to wake in the middle of the night crying, "I've done it, Tony! I've fixed that bitch for death! I've fixed her right up!" I have no doubt something is wrong with his state of mental health . . .

Of course neither Tony nor I could interpret his meaning. Only
on Frau von Bekken's death, several months later, did we begin to understand what he had done.

IV.

Extracted from The Avantguard Artists of the Nineteenth Century, *by W. B. Fry, London, William Heinmann, 1924:*

Enzio Savino (1864-1901)

Though certainly not the most successful, if success can be measured in terms of conventional fame, or monetary gain, Enzio Savino was possibly the most influential painter of the symbolist movement, surpassing even Redon and Moreau in influence amongst his fellow artists, and prestige amongst the culturally literate.

Born in Possagno, near Treviso, the son of a house painter, he was at a young age seduced by the German artist Ferdinand Keller, and moved with him to Paris in 1880, where he published his first series of lithographs *Concerto Campestre*, at the age of eighteen—a project that was undoubtedly financed by the purse of the older man.

Though not attending, he spent much of his time at the École des Beaux-Arts, where he made friends with Gerôme, by whom he was much admired, though to an equal degree feared. Carolus-Duran and Alexandre Cabanel, through uncontrollable jealousy and hate, had a petition passed around to ban Savino from the precincts of the school. The document stated that the young Italian was an evil influence on the other students and that his presence prevented them from going about their work. Savino slapped Cabanel in public and the latter challenged him to a duel. Savino, caring more for vengeance than honour, pulled out a *stiletto* and stabbed the teacher on the spot, though as luck would have it not mortally wounding him. After spending three months in jail, the young man was released, due to the influential intervention of Keller, who was still living in a nimbus of liquorice fascination.

His early work is vigorous and naturalistic (*cf. The Tree of the Hanged*, Bayerisches National Museum, Munich, 1883), but later his style became solemn and flushed with mythological influence, his subject matter for the most part being gleaned from ancient Egyptian and Greek lore. In 1884, he took part in the Salon des Indépendants, with high expectations of success. Unfortunately his work went largely unnoticed and was only praised by a few fellow artists. Enraged and frustrated, he tore his studio apart and left Paris. He was in debt to numerous persons, and involved in countless affairs of the heart. Needless to say, his sudden disappearance caused a great stir, and not a few friends to become enemies.

Many regarded him more in the light of a low adventurer than a skilled artist, and it must be said that his actions did much to form opinion in this wise. Edmond de Goncourt wrote: "He had the quasi savagery of all southern natures."

For nearly two years he was not heard of, and that period of his life is clouded in an almost resinous mystery. In Paris his name was heaped with ridicule, and rumours abounded. Some said that he had been seen in London, promenading between Piccadilly Circus and Hyde Park Corner; others claimed that he was in Germany, living at the expense of an immensely wealthy Baroness. Whatever the case, the year 1886 saw him reappear in Rome, a greatly changed man.

When he had left Paris, his personality had been that of a gifted guttersnipe. When he arrived in Rome, he did so as a man of culture—not subdued, for his nature was still as firey as ever—but one with greater knowledge, ability and inner strength.

He had acquired money. Not a great deal, but enough to dress like a gentleman and open up a studio on the Corso Magenta. In 1887 he exhibited at the Salon dell'Arte Metafisica, where he created a major stir with his *Night of Cain* (Städelsches Kunstinstitut, Frankfort). This grand canvas was his first major work and was hailed as a masterpiece. Wrote Adolfo de Carolis: "With that [*Night of Cain*] he showed us the path. He demonstrated how enormous difficulties might be cleared away with ease and made many great painters of the day tremble in despair [fearing] that they would lose the world's esteem."

That same year he produced over ninety canvases, including a number of works which today are regarded as some of his finest creations (*e.g. Arte Etiopica*, Museum of Art, Cleveland; *Minotaur*, Louvre, Paris; *Tribute to Exechia*, Wallraf-Richartz Museum, Colon).

V.

Excerpt from a police interview with mortician Gustave Schnittke by Konstable Hermann Bergen:

KB: . . . and tell me what happened at the wake.

GS: Well, if you're concerned about the condition of Chancellor von Bekken's honour, you would be better served asking Herr Doctor Ormand regarding the circumstances under which . . .

KB: The doctor is in custody, Herr Schnittke. We will question him soon. For now we need to hear your account of the events.

GS: I see. (pause) As you know, Frau von Bekken came to our facility early Wednesday morning.

KB: She visited?

GS: No, she was deceased. (pause) Doctor Ormand, who is, as you know, the family physician, brought in the body with the help of two attendants, both of whom left immediately following the completion of their grim delivery.

KB: Describe these two men.

GS: I do not know whether they were men or women. They were covered in black hoods and robes the way Italian body porters dress.

KB: They were Italian, you say?

GS: I could not see, due to the masks. They did not speak. They did not even grunt— Frau von Bekken was slight of frame as it is, and with the soul gone out of her . . .

KB: You are accusing the good *frau* of being soulless, Herr Schnittke?

GS: She was dead, of course she was soulless.

KB: This is what you mean?

GS: I have said so. May I continue?

KB: Please.

GS: Thank you. The family began to arrive about ten minutes later.

KB: And who was in attendance?

GS: I was getting to that, Konstable.

KB: Continue, Please.

GS: Frau von Bekken's daughter, Emilie, was

the first to arrive. She was accompanied by her fiancée, Wilhelm von Offenbach.

KB: Von Offenbach?

GS: From a little-known family, at least in the Chancellor's circle. A good enough lad— blond, green-eyed, just like his fiancée . . .

KB: Continue.

GS: Yes. Not long after . . .

KB: How long?

GS: Approximately four and a half minutes after Emilie and von Offenbach arrived, the Chancellor walked in with his military advisor, General Graf von Miltke, and the Reverend Helmuth Spier. The Reverend and the General created quite a stir when they entered the room, spewing invectives at one another right behind the poor Chancellor's back.

KB: Poor Chancellor? Is money an issue in this statement?

GS: (pause) The Chancellor was very sad, sir, as you can imagine one would be after losing one's spouse.

KB: Was he weeping?

GS: Freely.

KB: That is odd. I must make a note of it. Carry on.

GS: Emilie, her fiancée and Doctor Ormand . . .

KB: You speak in familiar terms of "Emilie"?

GS: I am an old family friend. I have known the good lady since she was a baby.

KB: Noted. We will speak of this later. Carry on.

GS: As I was saying, Emilie, von Offenbach and the doctor succeeded in shushing the bickering attendants. The Chancellor trudged over to the table on which his wife's body lay. He leaned down, tears in his eyes, to kiss her lips one last time. Suddenly, he stopped. A slight grunt escaped his throat, then his eyes widened as if a hammer of revelation had been brought down upon his skull . . .

KB: Spare us the dramatics.

GS: Er. (pause) The Chancellor looked quite surprised, then collapsed on the floor screaming, "*Mein Gott*! It's true! Ah, hellfire, it is true! Damn my soul, Spier, it's true!" Doktor Ormand ran and knelt by the Chancellor, trying to calm him, as Reverend Spier, looking rather puzzled, stooped down to look at the corpse's forehead.

KB: And what did he see, Herr Schnittke?

GS: The same thing I saw: words.

KB: Words. And what did these words say, Herr Schnittke?

GS: They said, "Here lies Salome, dreaming. The head in the museum her constant companion, wed for eternity in darkest hell. Mele Mele continues on the shores of darkness."

KB: And?

GS: Spier's reaction took us all by surprise. He stomped his feet about either side of the prone Chancellor, straddling him with his holy vestments, screaming at him. "I told you so, von Bekken, I warned you! Since you were barely off your mother's tits, I have warned you! 'Stay away from her,' I said, and, 'you have no interests in Africa'. But you persisted and now you have abetted your lusty *frau*'s eternal condemnation. Herod! HEROD!" he boomed as the chancellor lay there muttering and crying. His mind was quite gone by then, you know, and . . .

VI.

A few documents written by Savino to Wexler during the former's last months:

[Postcard]

December 29, 1900

Rome

Desperate. Send money!

[Letter]

January 10, 1901

Rome

Oh, you needn't be that way about it. I am absolutely miserable and you should have a little sympathy. If I say I need money, you can be damned well sure I do. As you know, the lawyers have a lean on my work and I cannot even set my hands on my past paintings, and I cannot set my hand to new projects for lack of funds. I need a new studio, paints, brushes, all sorts of things—or give me but a stick of charcoal and a bit of cloth and I will do you something for £1. Honesty my friend, things are getting to the edge. Do you know that I will be evicted from this room in a week? Well, it is true. So I tell you plainly: Hurry up and get me something SUBSTANTIAL to set myself right. *Seriously.*

E.

[Postcard]

February 1, 1901

Rome

I beg you to send me £20. Sick and miserable.

[Postcard]

February 8, 1901

Rome

Money. Money. Money.

(Isn't the picture on the front of this simply *absurd*!)

X.

Tattooed on the back of Enzio Savino:

Art-for-Art's-sake is no safe metier, not even for a prodigy such as he who under this, my stylus, bows in subjection. I embed in him, as my student again, the seeds of the fruition of my greatness, the scorpion's sting of stale vanity, of glory come and gone. May his fame, once invisible, again be manifest to those who never knew 'The Painter of Eyes'.

The Slug

I.

The ugliest of flowers are those reminiscent of dripping blood, with putrid scents—that smell like the unspoken and make one turn their head away in shame. Then there are monotonous white lilies or those agitated little cowards called anemones; and buzzing gentian and snot-like primrose; so many petals waiting to be covered in slime, as it is that certain minds are repulsed by blue skies and would much rather grovel than stand upright; tongue languishing, spilled out onto the ground, for a centipede to crawl over, for some snail to pass along.

II.

"No, it is not that. It is just that I don't feel my life is going in the direction that I wish."

"But you have a wonderful job."

"Which I am going to quit."

"Why?" Marcus asked. "You make almost twice as much money as I do."

"I have other opportunities," Dino replied. "And

there are more important things than making money."

He smiled. Involuntarily. He was a tall, very good-looking young man with broad shoulders, dark blond hair and soft brown eyes. His features were symmetrical.

"He has nice bone structure," a woman had once said of him.

"Well, you have always been fortunate," his friend, Marcus Hunziker, said now—somewhat thoughtlessly, since fortune is something that is not only intensively subjective, but also almost impossible to understand or calculate.

The glasses of Prosecco were emptied of their last drops.

The two men separated. Each went his own way.

Dino looked up at the cloudless sky and felt sad, at the flowers in the park and felt repulsed.

III.

The fact is that nothing is more valued in this world than banality.

IV.

He caught sight of a stooping, pigeon-chested man,

morphine-sedated, with a loose, flexible nose and ten fingers dangling to the ground. A hallucinating pedestrian. A shame, stinking like a urinal, hand now floating up, now extended to beg a coin.

Dino lay a five franc piece in that palm; wished it were his: grimy untrimmed nails and quivering digits; envied the ugly—bit his lip when he saw dwarves and felt intensely jealous of hunchbacks. Very short, balding men in baggy, ill-fitting pants fascinated him. Below average mammals. Hiccupping, stuttering idiots with social disabilities, cognitive dysfunctions, tumbling backward on the evolutionary scale.

V.

Some carnivorous fish; a city on fire.

VI.

He exercised as little as possible, purposefully stooped and went on a fried-foods diet; was attracted to women whose eyeliner was streaked along their cheeks; pleading psychological problems, day after day did not appear for work until, drawing his last pay-check, he was put on the unemployment roles, along with blind gardeners and women who scratched themselves as they mumbled about hard times.

VII.

The sky has the taste of disgust, screeching like an intoxicated cow or an old tire.

VIII.

The colour of vomit.

IX.

Dreamed: a metal cylinder, pollution, blue lakes raped by clouds of smut, dead fish flopping listlessly on the shore.

X.

Gradually his complexion began to change—to grow pasty, unhealthy. His teeth went from white to yellow, from yellow to green and his breath smelled like the oldest of cheese. His past seemed distant—galloping away like a horse hurling itself into hell.

XI.

He developed a taste for the cheapest wine—those vinegary distillations the litre bottles of which are unmarked by date—the types of grape poor pensioners drink so as to send their memories paddling off on thrifty lagoons populated by drowsy toads and featherless water birds. After drinking a few bottles of that liquid which was the tint of mule blood, eating a piece of liver fried in peanut oil, he would stroll off onto the piazza, sniff around the dresses of German tourists, swagger through the cafés, snatching up handfuls of potato chips from the counters, visiting remodelled urinals and subsequently striking up conversations with deaf widowers or young women who had grown fat on alpine cheese and who would deal with his advances by making guttural sounds and displaying mouthfuls of staggered teeth.

XII.

His smile looked like bloody sheep fat.

XIII.

"I am gaining ground," he drawled, as he looked at himself in the mirror.

XIV.

He searched out beings to befriend, took a train to Milan, scavenged in the gutters, picked up tramps with oozing flesh and drank horrible pale liquids with men who played dice in alleyways. Later, he would wake up on the edge of town, in some ditch and, after picking the earwigs and beetles out of his hair, wander to some road-side bar where he would stand a round to truck-drivers and those whores who hunt on the outskirts, pot-bellied women with muscular calves from much walking.

XV.

Indeed, progress he was making. His friends had fallen away from him, at first one by one—and then in mass. If one happened to see him approaching on the street, they would be sure to hurry away in order to avoid him—avoid the evil smell that came from his person, the depressing atmosphere that surrounded him like a sea of miasma.

XVI.

Women no longer smiled at him and, if he smiled at them, their usual rebuttal was "Disgusting!" which filled him with a satisfaction difficult to explain, but one which is probably not entirely unknown to our readers, who undoubtedly have at times felt a certain pride in the stench spewed out of their underarms, a certain smugness as their bellies grow larger and drag closer to the earth, stuffed as they are with old grease and new wine—the rinds of some unhealthy bit of cheese, the scrapings of a fry pan, or a few bites of mealy apple, a half moon of fermented citrus . . .

"Well, thank God for brothels," he said to himself.

Because the friends you pay for are certainly better than those who sanctimoniously claim to offer themselves selflessly. The friends you pay for will twist themselves into almost any position, stand on their heads, apply their outdated lips to your knuckles as you stuff a few worthy banknotes down their brightly-coloured and disordered brassieres.

XVII.

He wiggled his soft, slimy body into a pair of tight jeans.

XVIII.

A roaring crowd of maniacs biting each other's fingers off and afterwards drooling long strands of pink saliva which falls to the ground like webs as rockets go off overhead, lonely sparks expiring in overdoses of nausea.

XIX.

But everyone has their limit and it got to the point where even prostitutes of the lowest order refused to have him as a client—preferring starvation to his oily touch, to his demands which were too perverse even for those initiated in the darkest rites of fornication, and Dino, as passionate as any chamois or barnyard animal, was constrained to seek pleasure from knobby trees, sidewalk cracks and other inanimate objects of symbolic significance.

XX.

Passing by that stooping, pigeon-chested man; that stinking urinal, whose hand was extended for a few coins.

"You need to give to *me* now," Dino said.

"Eh?"

Dino began to ply through the man's pockets, located six or eight francs in change. The other was too high to offer resistance and our hero went off and spent the money on two glasses of beer at the Bar Apache and spoke to an old woman whose language he did not understand.

XXI.

Sometimes, when a tooth fell out of his rotting mouth, or he noticed how quickly he was growing bald, he would explode in tears of joy.

XXII.

When he walked, he made his way in unpleasant rhythmic waves, like a lingering camel.

XXIII.

A hunched over creature waddled down the street, a twenty cent cigar protruding from his loose, greasy lips, an aroma of the sewer hanging about his person

XXIV.

Everyone is vulgar.

Peter Payne

Tell zeal it wants devotion;
Tell love it is but lust;
Tell time it metes but motion;
Tell flesh it is but dust:
And wish them not reply,
For thou must give the lie.

—Sir Walter Raleigh

I.

A true crowd had gathered in front of the Tropicana Casino, upright livestock; harelips, evil odours, voices hatchet the air.

They were all packed against a temporary barrier like those used by police to keep back rioters. Red, white and blue banners hung from the light posts. Twenty-one white stretch limousines were parked side by side in the emptied section of the parking lot, ramps marking them off at either end like book ends. A stage had been set up, a big banner stretched across it saying in gold lettering:

KAPTAIN PETER PAYNE

*

A voice roared out over the speakers, "Ladies and

gentlemaaan! —Kaptain Petaaar Paaayne!!!"

The crowd cheered. Several whistles were audible.
A tri-coloured motorcycle spangled with stars buzzed
past, the rider waving. He wore a white leather outfit,
gold stripes jetting across. Men held small children on
their shoulders for a better view. The motorcycle turned
around, buzzed back, picking up speed, the rider popping a glorious wheely that made the crowd go wild.
At the end of the run the bike fishtailed, turned back,
front tire jacking up, him going the whole length of the
parking lot, all the while keeping only one hand on the
bike while he waved with the other. He road past, one
foot on the seat, one hand on the handle bars, the other
limbs outstretched like an acrobat (like Dennis Hopper
in *Easy Rider* . . . Paul Newman in *Butch Cassidy and
the Sundance Kid*). People were stirred, wanted this.
They smiled, wagged their heads enthusiastically and
cheered.

"He sure can ride," said a man, cowboy hat obscur-
ing his shrunken head.

A little girl stared at the spectacle with wide, impres-
sionable eyes.

Several young men covertly sipped cans of beer,
talking in low voices, their shoulders hunched.

Peter Payne whined up to the ramp several times,
testing the logistics. Finally he gave the thumbs up. He
would jump. The crowd became silent. He rode back a
couple of hundred yards. A small man in a mechanic's
jump-suit ran up to him. Everyone could see that they
were talking. Words exchanged. Gestures vehement.

The small man jogged away as Peter Payne revved up his bike. He waved and then buzzed toward the ramp, his motorcycle picking up speed. It hit the ramp and shot into the air. He let go of the handlebars, threw his arms over his head, quickly grabbed them again and he was on the other side. Cameras flashed. Sound issued from open mouths.

II.

Peter Payne was born in San Angelo, Texas. His father worked as a ranch hand. The family moved around, from Texas to Colorado, Colorado to New Mexico, then on to Nevada, Utah, Wyoming, Montana. His dad was a jack-of-all-trades, getting work where he could, drinking too much, getting fired, going straight, getting steady work, then hitting the bottle harder than ever. When he had money he spent it quickly, buying Peter and his older brother Jack whatever they wanted, even if it meant not paying the rent and bills. Mom bore with it, resigning herself to the wild ways of her man, Preacher.

He could hear his father outside howling at the moon, deep in liquor. Years later he would remember this with a kind of sacred awe, at the time he lay in his bed wide awake, his brother's breathing sounding out a comfort (their blood being the same) that could only be effaced by death.

The light shafted across the room and he lay on the

night, tv going low in the living room, Mom's pretty hair streaked with early grey. Preacher out there sitting on the tailgate, sipping Kentucky whisky, happy in the clean expanse and drink and speaking to those lavish stars.

III.

"Get your butt in that door!" Pete hissed.

Blaine sulked his way through the broad doors. The family found seats together in the sixth pew next to a very blond husband and wife with a teenage daughter yellow as straw.

Old women sat, gripping purses and bibles tightly, faces dry, pious, globbs of hunger and senility and protuberances of pain. Some newlyweds pressed close together, the man staring with animal satisfaction at his mate's swollen belly. Humbled fathers stared at the Aryan Christ before them, their eyes pink from Saturday night's twelve pack. A dirtyfaced boy murmured obscenities under his breath, Satan pricking within him, effing obsessive effs as the sanctuary filled its gut.

"Aren't they ever gonna start?" muttered Blaine. Virginia, Peter's wife, grabbed the boy's hand, squeezing it tightly so it hurt like hell.

"You kids need to learn a little religion," said Peter in a low voice. "When I was a boy I enjoyed church."

He lied.

"These days all these young people act like God for-saken atheists," commented the blond husband next to them.

Virginia nodded her head.

"Lizards," she mumbled.

A hush ran over the congregation. The pastor shuf-fled out, his small eyes taking silent count of his con-gregation. The organ broke in, hymn books shuffled, whispers were exchanged, *Bringing in the sheep* they sang, *Bringing in the sheep . . . We shall be rejoicing . . .*

Peter prayed to God.

Dear Lord, he prayed, *Dear Lord protect me and my family from harm's way. When I'm doing those stunts protect me so I will be able to be there for little Sarah and Blaine. And let Blaine see the light of Jesus. Let me be ok doing these stunts for seven more years and then I'll quit dear Lord. Praise be to Jesus Christ. Help me Christ, help me!*

IV.

Did Peter Payne have a definite perception of the validity of God?

No. He had faith in an occult substance, decidedly male but undefined, like a lump of clay. He saw afterlife vaguely, as a man half-blind sees the blurred image of his wife being violated as he struggles to release himself from the chair he is tied to. . . . Peter Payne saw God as something separate from himself. He did not consider that God (sitting cross legged atop a pile of shit) created man and the world as a spider does its web. . . . The cruciform speck of gold which hung from his neck was to him not so much the logo of the Eternal as it was of White Honour. . . . It showed that any homosexual tendencies he had were most likely latent, his money was not acquired through cheating people, his sins were washed clean by virtue of their having been performed under the auspices of European ancestry. The Lord was an ethereal substance which he allowed to molest him, as an altar boy does a priest. Man without God would be like an octopus without a saddle, pumpkin pie without horseradish, a chimney without a negligee . . .

V.

"Come on you son of a bitch!" Virginia cried out as she fed the machine another silver dollar.

All around the vibrant clink of coinage rang out. Money was falling in heaps. Lights went off, sirens sounded. Undoubtedly many were becoming rich at that very moment. A woman walked by, her shirt front filled with silver, her white belly dipping a little over the rim of her pants. Cigarettes burned in every mouth: Pall Mall, Marlboro, Lucky Strike, Camel: straights, menthol, lights, 100's.

"I've got an addictive personality," Virginia would

tell people.

She lived to eat. Gambling was a hunger. The buffets at the casinos were phenomenal, gross. Roast beef floated in a thin gravy spotted with white clots of fat. Baked cod, chippy and chewy, a faint taste of sewage to the meat. Fried chicken, the crust aged, effete, a reservoir of oil hidden beneath the skin. Vegetables embalmed in a lukewarm broth, all vitamins judiciously leached from their fibres. Desserts bright, tall, towering, colourful, silicon sweet.

Bellies distended, rumps hanging low, aqueous, they make their way back to grey moneylust, mud, noxious, grey smoke sifting through their ears, packing against their craniums, hair follicles.

VI.

Dad is a motorcycle daredevil. Watch out. If he dies that means no him. So I don't want to pray. I don't want to pray not because I don't want Dad to be OK, but because I don't want to. I don't want to be stabbed by a spirit, but I don't want to pray, be bored and pray. Before dinner I just pretend (head bent, churlish, as a criminal might submit to the lash of a whip, inwardly defiant). Mom might whoop me, but I don't care. I'm Blaine. I don't care. Because I am not a sweet boy or a sissy and I knew but did not know, wanted but would not believe, would not admit.

It was early morning and I was walking down the hall. I needed to go so I was walking down the hall and then I heard that scream and did not consider. Did not consider who it was but I knew it was a pain yell, like a real pain and it could have been her. So I opened the door and there was a man hurting her, his back arched up and the skin like it was wet. She was screaming and he was hurting her. He was on top of her and hurting her and then yelled at me and told me to get out. His face was red, not just angry red but like he had been holding his breath, and it was not like I had ever seen it before, but it was Dad, a stranger yet him. Nobody said anything about it, just as if it had never happened. She seemed OK and I didn't say anything about it. She must not have been hurt too bad because she was in a good mood and made pancakes and bacon and joked and moved around with her big thighs filling out the kitchen. I just hoped she wasn't hurt bad somewhere I couldn't see. Because Dad could hurt you bad if he wanted to. I know he could. His arms could hurt you. I don't care though because I don't care if I get hurt. I don't care (it being that this very pain that his mother bore, whirling of blood, tempest of milk and okra, was the agony he felt, being pulled from the other side, mysterious pre-existence-natal-wrack— attracted by the odour of blood, semen—into the fleshy folds of the womb, tortured, shot out, a victim of raw elements, irreversible laws of universal suffering).

VII.

"Look Merle, you better go home. I don't need any drunks on my team. Any boy that's with me needs to be square. You get it?"

"Sure Pete, I get it."

"You know, you come over and start helping me to set things up and you're all boozed, or even just got yourself a bad hangover, and that's no good. I'm going to need you tomorrow, so I want you to be in good shape."

"Pete, you know I love you. I'll listen Pete. You know I don't mean to drink so much. I'll make it OK Pete. Don't worry, I'll make it OK."

"I hope so Merle. By God I hope so."

Peter could not help but get nervous when he caught Merle on a drunk. There was no question that Merle was a good mechanic; and a decent technician provided he was sober.

"That drinking problem's a terrible thing," Peter would say. "My brother had it and it is a terrible thing."

My brother had it and my father had it, he thought, *but it killed my brother. Preacher was big and of another time and was a match for it or at least a contender. You watch Merle, he told himself, because contender he is not.*

*

Phoenix, AZ
10:30 PM

The night before a jump.

Payne climbs into his air stream. He eats cold cereal while listening to music and then goes to bed.

3:30 AM

Peter Payne wakes to the sound of water. He arises. Merle is standing in the kitchenette peeing on the stove. He is not sober.

VIII.

"Virginia, what the hell is this? I got the statement from the bank today and according to it there's five-thousand dollars less in our savings account than there's supposed to be!"

"Well Petey . . ." Virginia started.

"Don't Petey me Virginia. It's that damned gambling of yours, isn't it? Hell, I knew it was getting out of control. You go down to those God damned casinos and flush my money down the toilet, don't you? . . . I'm out there risking my neck—literally risking my God damned neck—to earn some money so me and you and Blaine and Sarah can have a decent middle-class life, and what are you doing but just flushing it all down the toilet!"

"Oh Pete!" Virginia cried, breaking down.

She collapsed at his feet, burying her head in his trouser leg. Tears danced onto his shoe.

"You've done wrong Virginia, you've done wrong. . .

. You're just letting yourself go and I really don't know what to do about this. . . . You need help. . . . You know you need some God damned help."

"I know I do. I know I do Pete."

IX.

"Why doesn't that man have a wife?" she would ask.

"Just look at him," Peter would inevitably reply. "What female is going to take a man like that?"

"Well, men without women worry me."

No one in fact had ever seen Merle hand in hand with a woman. When the boys would start talking about the female anatomy he would keep silent, even blush slightly. Yet his squalid little apartment was littered with objectionable literature. His mind was obviously not devoid of carnal thought. No one suspected him of being a saint.

X.

I bet he sins. I bet he sins more than me. Mom calls me a sinner. She's fat but I'm a sinner. She drinks pop. Merle doesn't have a cross around his neck like Dad does connecting him to life. I better watch out that I don't turn out like him. He always smells bad so my nose wants to run away. I don't want to smell like that. Dad smells good. Because he's got that cross I guess connecting him to grass and baked things and I didn't kill Christ, I swear it wasn't me though I'm going to sin I know but I'm going to smell good.

XI.

Virginia was blowing up, bloating out, tearing the seams of her clothes, making eyebrows rise. She had had a nice figure when they had first met. It was not having two kids that killed it. It was her addiction to food and soda, her mad chase after calories. The fat had no place to go. Her asthma prevented her from much in the way of exercise. Peter found himself cringing before her naked body, caressing it with little enthusiasm. For him bedroom activity became a regular chore. He put her on a diet. He was sick of seeing her tremendous rump wagging around the house.

"No more pop and junk food," he said.

"I don't eat junk food. I eat people food."

"That's right, you eat people food. Enough for about two or three people. Now it's time for person food. Singular. You get it?"

That night at supper he shook his head when she started helping herself to seconds of the pineapple whip.

"What's that got in it? Marshmallows, cottage cheese. That's no diet food! If you're still hungry eat some more salad."

"Rabbit," Virginia mumbled under her breath as she stabbed her fork into a leaf of lettuce.

*

She lay beneath the covers, a paperback novel in one hand. His back was to her. He lay curled up on his side, eyes closed.

Why doesn't he ever make love to me? she thought. *I have desires just like every other woman. More probably. He needs to know what I want . I'll give him a hint. I'll ask him if he feels like doing anything.*

"So what do you feel like doing honey?" she said.

"Sleeping."

She put down her book and began to caress his shoulder. She began kissing his neck, reaching her hand around him and running it around his stomach thinking *honey come on and turn over my wants and needs with your steam because I don't like being the way I'm not supposed to* and him slowly opening his eyes believing *must turn over and do my sacred duty be squeezed as if by a python back-breaker me nailed to a cross well it's only a bed.*

XII.

If his brother could visit this man, he, Peter Payne. This man so unlike that boy who had been there wide awake while their father had howled at the moon. . . . This man, children branching off him like strange, somewhat problematic fruit, a heavy woman brushing up against him in the night. . . . A man performing cryptic adult rituals, succumbing to social shackles, living behind a brutally handsome face. He was far from what he had been, as a pile of greasy sausage is far from the pig it once was, comfortably wallowing in the mud.

Jack sat there in his trailer cleaning his guns, the swimsuit model pinned to the wall, her breasts full and uptilted, water rolling off her brown, apparently desirable body, insensitive, paper, the room without joy. There was the bottle and he would drink from the bottle, and there was the Horse and Hunt Club and the shooting and there was Peter and memories of violation, tubes of red, jungles of gleaming nerve.

I tried to keep his spirits up, he thought. *You tried,* he told himself. *You tried but you did not give more of yourself than you thought was essential. You blew it man; hard. Validate all you like, but you blew it and can only pray to Jesus Christ for forgiveness and hope and pray for heaven.*

And then there was the field of white fingers, parade of turf, choking agitation, underground rivers of distilled flesh, rolling to outlet.

XIII.

Virginia begins to receive mail from the casinos regularly: pamphlets, propaganda. She masks her habit, fabricates stories about where the family money goes, tells bottomless lies, bribes her children in order to keep their mouths shut. She rotates between the tv and the refrigerator, grows fat, stupid, lazy, indentured to greenbacks.

"Meatloaf! Are you joking?" Peter says at the dinner table. "This is the third night running. Not to mention the fact that you use so many breadcrumbs the stuff belongs in a bakery. Where is the prime rib? Are we paupers? Have I been chasing the American dream in order to eat mystery meat?"

Virginia laughs it off. She can pass almost anything off as meat. She is clever that way. Still, the money she is managing to save by feeding her family scraps hardly makes up for that which is sucked down by the slot machines. She runs down to the casinos the moment Peter is out the door. She gambles away whatever she can get her hands on, never stopping to think how big the odds are against her.

XIV.

"Twenty-five limousines side to side is what, about two-hundred foot?" said Merle. "When you did twenty-one last year you didn't have much room to spare as I recall, so I don't see . . ."

"We just need to change the dynamics of the jump," said Payne. "Make the ramps more effective. . . . Hell, I can figure it out."

*

He prayed frequently, planned. Pictured a flour-white Jesus before him, rallying him across the twenty-five limos with the magical power of Christianity. The image would become distorted: Jesus appearing with a turned up, lop-sided nose . . . his hair black, curly . . . lips grinning sarcastically.

Peter made mental offerings to the deity in order to placate him. He had managed to arrive at a satisfactory agreement with God before a jump, laying his children, wife and faith at the altar of monotheism. His courage was largely based on a belief in the divine presence; in divine protection.

He kneeled in prayer, hands clasped, head bowed. It was a Tuesday afternoon, the church was nearly empty. A woman several pews behind him fanned herself with a pamphlet. He felt sticky, uncomfortable down to his loins. He poured forth his heart to Jesus Christ, an awful plaster statue, a ludicrous piece of trash. Vehement, like an idol worshipping savage he prayed, coppery taste in mouth, anus contracted, lips pressed tense.

He got up and remembered how it was. *His station wagon was there*, he thought, *and I can't say I knew because I don't know what I knew, just felt something and did not even bother to knock and opened up and went in. You felt something*, he told himself. *You felt something and had been feeling it for a long time and it was like you always knew what kind of a seed he was and you could smell it all rotten like puke.*

There was that smell and the mellow buzzing of flies in the heat of the trailer and a sense of decay and sadness, even when you go through a dead man's clothes years later, not rotten but subtle odour and were told and crashed in the belly of water.

XV.

"Pete's not here right now. I don't know when he'll be back. You're welcome to wait for him if you want though. . . . It's just me and Sarah here. Blain is off spending the night at a friend's house," said Virginia.

"That sounds fine," said Merle sitting down.

Sarah lay on the rug watching television.

Virginia had been inwardly lamenting the fact that she was cut off from the casino for the night. She had $300 in her pocketbook that her husband knew nothing about . . . To see this money multiply, thicken substantially . . . That's pleasure . . . For each dollar to give birth to ten . . . Sarah was the only obstacle . . . Yet Merle . . . She could leave her . . .

"Say Merle," said Virginia. "You wouldn't by any chance be willing to babysit Sarah here for an hour or so while I take a run to the store, would you? There's beer in the fridge and food and you could drink beer and watch TV and watch her until I get back."

Sarah looked up sleepily, forehead wrinkled, dissatisfied.

"No, I don't mind," replied Merle. "I'm sitting here anyhow. . . . You go ahead. She'll be here when you get back."

Hearing the door slam his heart ticked. He went to the refrigerator and opened a can of beer. Sarah was falling asleep. He sat back down and watched as her eyelids sunk.

"She's asleep," he said aloud. "I better take her to bed."

He picked her little body up in his arms. Her mouth dropped open, the chapped mouth of a child, like a wound on her face. . . . Laying her down on the mattress. . . . An innocent room, wallpaper spotted with balloons of basic colours, red, yellow, blue.

He watched her breath. . . . Face puffing, perspiring, his nostrils quivering. . . . It was only later that he would think, *I'm such a coward, such a God damned coward* believing *when that tree grew tall and man lazy could no longer climb it only fit for the axe then there is the grandeur of being hated and self-hated some dish left out to rot if only I too could fly through the air a condor.*

Yet whatever was dirty, volatile about his nature . . .

She lay innoxious, emblematic (to him) of his own social inadequacy, venery, that moment of crime, an explosion of filth, that irreversibly severs all cords of virtue, exposes man as a spineless amphibian living off the carcasses of ladybugs and butterflies, melting their delicate wings between tongue and teeth.

Peter came home and Merle was sitting on the couch drinking a beer and Virginia was not there, but Sarah was in her room already, and the man who rode the motorcycle said angry words about his wife.

XVI.

Peter Payne spent the day in his trailer in quiet contemplation. At noon he walked around the jump site, inspected the ramp, looked out over the parking lot where they would be. When a reporter asked him if he was prepared to go through with it he replied, "Well I've got certain contracactory obligations so, like it or not, I've got to just go ahead and do it." Early in the evening he ate a light meal, alone, but the Salisbury steak was without flavour and he did not have faith in it.

When the time came he put on his leather outfit, took up his helmet and went out to his bike. Merle informed him that it was in condition.

*

The incalculable eyes of night laughed, rockets shot up spraying mallow, lilac, mauve . . . popping, crackling. . . . An odour of sulfur tinged the air. The human animals once again gathered around to see, as wolves might gather around the glow of a dying fire.

"Hell," said Merle. "This'll be a hell of a jump." There was tension, naked, breathed, yes, them. Their white faces formed a wall of worm-like countenance, the many arms and legs postured, gestured accordingly, as some strange satanic beast, teeth shining through the slash of lips, red tongues moist, flickering.

Once again Peter Payne rides out. A wheelie. Cheers.

He gathers strength by riding back and forth before the people, one wheel jacked up in the air, his white uniform dramatically patriotic, warrior-like. He accepts the gurgle of praise. He has a love of his fans, the American people, an attachment to them, he would verily throw his body at their mercy.

Eyes viewing the universe through the visor of his helmet, an armour of leather covering his skin—no inch of epidermis showed out of this shell. These acts performed on the dust of the earth assumed Gargantuan proportion, truly epic, immortal, as a star at dawn, larvae. The disembodied voice of the announcer rang out describing in clean masculine tones the madness of the event.

Once again Payne goes through the motions of testing the jump, riding up on the ramp, viewing the cars before him. He gives the thumbs-up.

"So that's it?" Merle asks running up.

"It's as it as it's going to be," says Peter Payne.

Amidst the hush of the fans his bike screams toward the ramp, angling up it. He shoots into the air, over limousines, yet falling short of the opposite ramp, the other shore so to speak, his front tire hits the front hood of the next to last car, slipping, the man's body hurled violently against the pavement, hands still clinging to the bike as it comes after him, bouncing against his back and twisting away.

XVII.

What was his view of reality?

It was not mundane in the absolute sense of the word. He superimposed the mythopoeic vision of God on the corporeal world, lending his life that essence of naiveté necessary to soar above the common strains. His thought patterns stemmed from a definite ego, not altogether catholic, which subordinated certain glories as fixed property for him alone. The honour of the male Homo sapiens naturally tinged his environment; the habits inherited from the ape naturally lent his outlook the perfume of brutality. He saw the world through the fog of the Western Anglo, subliminal frequencies transmitting silhouettes of cowboys, victorious soldiers, tattered flags, hitchhikers on lone prairies, longhorns—all overlapping, American in label.

How did he, Mr. Payne, think?

His initial reaction to situations produced images, calling on his storehouse of previous impressions, prejudices, inherent tendencies. These coagulated into calculations, emotions, shocks that impelled his person forward, to perform tasks, jump cars, pray to Christ, penetrate his wife. His thoughts co-ordinated themselves according to his geographic location. The United States appeared against the panorama of the universe as immense, far outsizing suns, solar systems, how much more so opposing countries. The Witness watched within, relatively indifferent, clean, apart from the vile places Peter's hands went, performing his mortal functions of defecation and procreation. The laughter, the agony of his life, were lines penned in the air, fruits bit into bursting like bubbles. His thoughts were countless, sordid, grand, sleazy, ambitious, pitiful. He thought often.

Did he love his family?

He loved his son and daughter by ties of kinship, as one loves one's country. He loved his wife conjugally, originally with attachment and sexual passion, as a source of gratification, later only in the sense of the actual physical action (almost as a commandment).

Was he afraid?

No.

XVIII.

I heard her crying in the middle of the night, but I didn't say anything because I had heard Dad tell Merle that no one could understand women and Merle said that only pink sissies could, his voice blurpy like a toad's and his hair all strung on his scalp like a doll's. She's just a little girl, but I bet she will be a funny woman. So she didn't come because they kept saying that she was traumatized but I went into the elevator and pressed six and did not wait to hear. They told me at the desk what room he was in and then the nurse saw I didn't know and took me past the machines and in there. There was just the white cast like a mummy, like something from the movies but I saw his eyes and knew he was in there because they were looking at me. They were bright and true blue and he looked at me. He couldn't move because of all those casts. He wasn't dead because he was looking at me, because he talked to me, or made sounds that I understood when I listened close. He said he bet that I didn't want to ride a bike any more. I told him I did. They say wages are bad. I am Blaine so I don't want to work for wages. He's old and he won't do anything any more. That's probably that punishment. I should not care. I'm Blaine so I should not care. I'm a brick.

Also from Chômu Press:

Looking for something else to read? Want a book that will wake you up, not put you to sleep?

The Dracula Papers, Book I: The Scholar's Tale
By Reggie Oliver

Revenants
By Daniel Mills

Nemonymous Night
By D.F. Lewis

The Man Who Collected Machen and Other Weird Tales
By Mark Samuels

The Great Lover
By Michael Cisco

For more information about these books and others, please visit: http://chomupress.com/

Subscribe to our mailing list for updates, news and exclusive rarities.

Publishing History

Versions of the following stories in this volume were originally published in other places:

'Collapsing Claude' was originally published in *Flesh and Blood*

'The Dancing Billionaire' was originally published in *Harpur Palate*

'Brother of the Holy Ghost' was originally published in *The Journal of Experimental Fiction*

'Maledict Michela' was originally published in *Nemonymous*

'The Life of Captain Gareth Caernarvon' was originally published in *McSweeney's*

'The Chymical Wedding of Des Esseintes' was originally published in *Cinnabar's Gnosis*

'The Search For Savino' was originally published in *Neotrope*

'Peter Payne' was originally published in *RE:AL, The Journal of Liberal Arts*

About the Author

Brendan Connell was born in Santa Fe, New Mexico, in 1970. He has had fiction published in numerous places, including *McSweeney's*, *Adbusters*, *Fast Ships, Black Sails* (Nightshade Books, 2008), and the World Fantasy Award winning anthologies *Leviathan 3* (The Ministry of Whimsy, 2002), and *Strange Tales* (Tartarus Press, 2003). His other published books are: *The Translation of Father Torturo* (Prime Books, 2005*), Dr. Black and the Guerrillia* (Grafitisk Press, 2005), *Metrophilias* (Better Non Sequitur, 2010), and *Unpleasant Tales* (Eibonvale Press, 2010).

Lightning Source UK Ltd.
Milton Keynes UK
08 January 2011

165354UK00001B/5/P